Nocturnal Nightmares

Melody Grace

NOCTURNAL NIGHTMARES

Copyright © 2019 by M.G.M Publishing.

All rights reserved. Printed in the United States of America. No part of this book may be used or reproduced in any manner whatsoever without written permission except in the case of brief quotations em—bodied in critical articles or reviews.

This book is a work of fiction. Names, characters, businesses, organiza—tions, places, events and incidents either are the product of the author's imagination or are used fictitiously. Any resemblance to actual persons, living or dead, events, or locales is entirely coincidental.

For information contact :
https://www.facebook.com/nocturnalnanny

Cover design by Victoria Davies @VC_BookCovers
Illustrations by: Aina & Christian Tolero @hoomanerror
Interior by E.P. Boyr & Melody Grace
Edited by Nick Botic & E.P. Boyr

ISBN: 9781072356233

First Edition: October 2019

10 9 8 7 6 5 4 3 2 1

Dedicated to my son, Logan: Mommy will always chase away your bad dreams, even if she creates them from her stories. I love you so much, Bub.

I would also love to say a special thank you to all my friends, family, and fans. None of this would be possible without each and every one of you!

CONTENTS

NOCTURNAL NANNY 2

THE CHICUBARI 27

THE CEMETERY 36

SIX MINUTES 41

GRACIE 44

SOMEONE IS STEALING MY STORIES 50

DAYDREAMS 55

THE BEK 61

THE PRICE OF A SOUL 67

FORGOTTEN THOUGHTS 72

MY HOUSE IS HAUNTED 76

CANNIBAL CONFESSIONS 81

THE STALKER 83

WE WILL RETURN 87

THE DREAM WHISPERER 93

THE FAIRY GARDEN 102

UNKNOWN NUMBER 106

NANNY 129

- COLD BLOODED 135
- ANIMAL CONTROL 140
- DON'T FORGET TO BREATHE 153
- ARACHNOPHOBIA 157
- THE FLORIST 159
- IT WAS ALWAYS MEREDITH'S FAULT 163
- LOVE, THE EASTER BUNNY 168
- MY BIGGEST FAN 171
- I'M TURNING INTO A BEE 176
- GRAVITY HILL 179
- SWEET TOOTH 183
- YOU CAN NEVER BE TOO CAREFUL 188
- CAKE 191
- PAST LIVES 198
- MR. LAKAVOTE 202
- THE TEA PARTY 208
- YOU DON'T EVEN KNOW 212
- NOCTURNAL NIGHTMARES 215
- EVERYONE HAS SECRETS, WHAT'S YOURS? . 219
- THE SHADOWS OF SUNNY HOLLOW 225

WOMEN MUST SERVE MEN	*230*
ACKNOWLEDGMENTS	*236*
ABOUT THE AUTHOR	*237*

Nocturnal Nanny

part one

𝓘 HAVE BEEN A NANNY GOING ON fifteen years now.

I love what I do, most of the time. What I am about to share with you though, is the "rest of the time". These are my accounts of the strange encounters that have happened to me over the years, and that are very much still happening. I will be changing the names of the children and myself for privacy reasons, and each following part will represent a different family.

The Cook Family

I had been hired by the Cook family for exactly five minutes before I realized something about their house was off.

It was fairly large, with many rooms and hidden features. One room had a small door you could walk through and end up at the other end of the house due to a small passageway behind the walls.

The Cooks told me the house had been a hideaway for some drug lords, and they got a great deal on the price due to it being foreclosed. There was an intercom in every room connecting them to each other, which I thought was kind of cool. I could talk to the kids while they were playing in another room while I did some household chores.

I met the children shortly after arriving. They had a four-year-old girl named Carly, and a two-year-old boy named Emmett. They were both very polite and appeared to be well behaved: score!

The parents left for an evening while I watched them on a trial basis—you know, to make sure it would be a good fit. This is when I found that it wasn't just the house that was strange.

Carly's room was downstairs. I heard her playing on the intercom and talking to someone. I didn't think anything of it until she told whoever it was that they were going to be in trouble if they did "that".

I made my way down the stairs and back into her room. When I got there I couldn't believe my eyes. Her mattress had been thrown across the room and her dresser had been pushed so that it was facing the window.

In shock, I asked her how she had done all of this and why? Carly turned to me, shrugged, and replied, "He was all in white!"

Goosebumps emerged all over my entire body. I felt cold … very cold. Carly had acted like everything was normal, and that made the situation even more terrifying.

When their parents arrived home, I didn't mention the room incident and left, unsure if I would return. Once at home that night, I'd come to the conclusion that Carly was just messing with me. I would take that job after all.

I returned to the house the next day and nothing strange happened; there was no mention of the man in white. It went on like this for a while until one day I arrived and upon entering I got the dreadful feeling that something was wrong.

At about 2:00 p.m., I placed them both down for a nap; Emmett slept upstairs in his room, and Carly downstairs in hers.

Around 2:30 p.m. I heard scratching on the wall.

The Cooks didn't have any pets, so I figured maybe it was some wild animals next to a window or something.

About two minutes later I heard it again.

Scratch, scratch, scratch.

I got up to investigate, but it stopped as soon as I walked into the kitchen. So, I went back to folding the laundry in the other room and listened. After the first scratch, I jumped up and ran to the kitchen. That's when I saw that the intercom was lighting up from Carly's room.

I crept down the stairs and peeked inside. Carly was snoring away, clearly sleeping heavily. I started to walk back up the stairs when I heard the scratching again, still coming from her room. Before I could turn around, I heard Carly say, "Shhh! Gordon, I'm sleeping!"

I booked it back up those stairs and finished the laundry.

The scratching sounds never came back that day, or any other day.

Weeks went by. Odd little things continued to happen here and there during my time with the kids—toys would appear in weird places; the kids would talk to imaginary friends often, especially one named Gordon; Emmett would zone out, staring at the wall for minutes at a time; the sound of footsteps would come from upstairs while we were all downstairs; music from an old toy would come from one of the hidden rooms in the basement; and doors that I had previously shut would open, especially the one leading to the basement.

All these occurrences happened often, almost daily. I chalked them up to being the sounds of an old house and kids being kids, but nothing prepared me for the pictures.

Every day, I would have arts and crafts with them and every day, among other drawings, they would both draw the same picture. It's a little hard to describe, because I had never seen anything like it before, but it was a design that seemed to go on forever, and in the middle of the design was a small stick-like figure of a man. Every day, same design, same figure, drawn by both kids.

The oddest part was Emmett's drawing. He was two years old and this design was that of an older kid, yet he drew it with such precision it was astonishing, especially when all his other doodles and crafts were that of a two-year-old's level. I asked them almost every day what the design meant. They would be in a trance-like state while drawing it, and after would have no recollection of doing it or what it was.

Even with all the strange things that seemed to happen daily, I continued to nanny for the family until one cold afternoon.

That day left me running for the door, never to return.

The leaves on the trees outside their home had started to fall, which meant winter was just around the corner. I had put the kids down for a nap a little early that day due to them complaining about being "too sleepy to keep their eyes open".

I was enthralled in a good book by the fireplace when I heard someone walking up the stairs from Carly's room. I called out to her, told her it wasn't time to wake up yet and to go back to bed. The footsteps continued up the stairs and into the kitchen. I called out to her again, told her to try to go back to sleep and that I would wake her in an hour.

I was looking at the hallway, waiting for her to walk into the room, when I heard running coming from the opposite direction.

Key word: *heard*.

I saw absolutely nothing run across that hallway, but I definitely heard it. I ran down after her, still trying to figure out how she had not only passed by without me seeing, but had turned around and passed by *again*.

When I got to her room, I abruptly opened the door, but when I peered inside Carly was sound asleep. I walked back up the stairs into Emmett's room to check on him. He was sound asleep, as well. That's when I heard the voice, clear as day. It was right behind me, whispering into my ear, *"Leave now!"*

I immediately woke up both kids, telling them I had decided we would play in the front room until their parents arrived home, and kept my eye on the front door the entire time.

I can't really recall what we were playing or how long I sat there waiting, because I just wanted to leave.

And that was my last day as the Cooks' nanny.

part two

The Johnson Family

$\mathcal{D}$ESPITE MY ALARMING EXPERIENCE WITH the Cooks, I decided to post an ad on a local page to offer my nanny services to others. I figured this way I could vet the families better before I accepted the job.

After a few days of receiving random inquiries that would not fit my schedule, a promising one came in.

This is the message I received:

> *Hello Miss Fraser,*
>
> *My wife and I are looking for a part-time nanny Monday through Wednesday from 7:00 a.m. to 3:00 p.m.*

We have one half-child who is five years old and very well behaved. She's really no bother at all; practically takes care of herself. All she needs is an adult present to make sure she eats at the right time and doesn't go outside.

I know this may seem a little odd, but she is ... diabetic and has an allergy to the sun. If we sound like a good fit, please feel free to email us back! We will be in touch to set up a time to meet.

Sincerely,

The Johnsons

Now I know what you're thinking. What in the world is a half-child, right? Well, I can tell you at this point I sincerely have no idea. I really needed a job and figured it was just a typo in the email. Especially since the rest sounded so promising.

I immediately sent them a reply and waited to hear back.

Within ten minutes, I received a reply with their address, phone number, and a time to come by the following day to meet them.

Apparently, they needed a nanny just as much as I needed a job.

The next day, I drove to the address given and was stunned at the sight before me when I pulled up. It was the most beautiful house I had ever laid my eyes on. (I say "house" very loosely as it was more like a freaking *mansion*—beautiful Victorian-style four-story home with a gorgeous wrap-around porch and a breathtaking garden on the side.)

When I approached the steps, the door immediately whipped open and out stepped a woman I assumed to be Mrs. Johnson. She embraced me in an awkward hug and told me how excited she was to meet me while leading me inside.

Upon entering, I was assaulted by an overpowering, sickly sweet smell. Also ... everything inside the home was spotless, perfect—too perfect.

Mr. Johnson gave me a firm handshake as he welcomed me to their home. I saw a little girl hiding behind him and assumed it was their daughter. As I bent down to greet her, Mr. Johnson told me her name was Margaret. She looked like an antique porcelain doll, all dressed up in a Victorian-style dress with perfect blonde curls and big blue eyes.

They gave me a quick tour of the house and handed me a list of Margaret's schedules along with some instructions as we walked. I looked it over quickly; it seemed very detailed and precise but not too difficult. As we made our way back to the front room, we sat down and discussed what other duties the job would entail and what I would be paid. Since they were offering me double what I made for the Cooks, I eagerly accepted.

They were thrilled and told me I would start the next day.

Margaret tugged on her father as I was leaving and asked if I would be staying longer than her last nanny did. Mr. and Mrs. Johnson exchanged nervous glances, then told her it would depend on her, whatever that meant.

I waved goodbye and returned home.

The next day, I arrived fifteen minutes early to get settled. I wanted to familiarize myself with the place before they left. They assured me everything would be great and that they had a good feeling about this.

With that, they kissed Margaret goodbye, gave me a nervous wave, and left.

The first thing I needed to do after they were gone was go the fridge and find what was needed to prepare Margaret's breakfast. This is where things got a little strange.

Inside the fridge were prepackaged meals stacked on top of each other, a time stamp on each one. I pulled out the one on top to inspect it. It was a mushed mess of brownish-red goo, and after opening it up I realized it looked exactly how it smelled: awful.

I placed it in a bowl and set it on the table as the Johnson's instructed and called Margaret in to eat.

When she sat down, she looked at me awkwardly and asked me if I was going to set the timer and leave.

What?

Confused, I grabbed the list of instructions and, sure enough, right at the top it said to set a timer for Margaret to eat. Then I was to leave the kitchen and lock the door behind me. I'll admit, that made me really uncomfortable. I started to wonder just what I had gotten myself into, but I did what they asked; I set the timer and left, locking the door behind me.

Fifteen minutes later, the bell went off.

Margaret tapped on the door to be let out.

As I opened it, I half expected to find the kitchen a mess. Instead I found it exactly how I'd left it and the bowl of whatever she'd been eating was gone. Margaret grabbed my hand and said it was time to play now.

Her parents were right; she was an easy child. Very polite, well behaved, and she made the time go by fast with her active imagination.

That afternoon, as we were playing with her dolls, I heard a knock on her bedroom door. When I got up to answer it, Margaret tugged me back down and told me we weren't allowed to answer it and to just ignore it. Confused once again, I pulled out the notes I had tucked in my pocket, and once again the answer was right there on the list.

Never answer any knocks.

I nervously looked back at Margaret. She was back to playing like nothing had happened. At this point, I was starting to think that maybe I was simply destined to work for peculiar families. After all, my experiences thus far had been anything but normal.

When she was done playing with her dolls, Margaret excitedly jumped up and walked over to her bookshelf, asking me if I would read to her. After she grabbed a book that looked like a journal, she plopped down in my lap and opened it up. Inside there were photographs of random people taped to the pages. No names, no writing, just pictures. I asked her who they were and she said that I had to make up a story for each one. Feeling really uncomfortable, I asked her if we could read another book instead. She sighed, took the album back from me, and grabbed another book.

Around noon, Margaret started to get unruly (I assumed because lunch was coming up). Once again, I went to the fridge and repeated the steps from that morning; putting the gooy redish mess in a bowl, setting the timer, and locking the door behind me. After she was done, she ran up the stairs and told me she needed some alone time.

Sure kid, I thought to myself, and decided to do some exploring.

I entered one of the rooms in the house that I determined was most likely a lounge area. In the back of the room was a huge library with a river of books loaded onto the shelves. As I approached it, I heard an identical knock to the one from Margaret's room earlier. I listened closely, and realized it was coming from behind the bookshelf. As soon as I put my ear up to it, Margaret rushed in the room and shouted, *"No!"*

I turned to face her just in time to feel a sharp pain radiate from my hand.

Yes, the little shit actually bit me.

Looking down at my hand, I noticed two small puncture wounds dripping with blood.

I glared at Margaret—even though she genuinely did look apologetic—and sent her to her room. She stomped off with as much attitude as a five-year-old could muster.

I walked to the bathroom to find a first aid kit.

As I was searching I, half-jokingly, thought I should look at the notes I was left to see if this was covered in them.

It was.

At the bottom of the page it said:

If Margaret bites you, immediately call us.

I picked up my phone, called Mrs. Johnson, and told her what had happened. She told me to hurry up to her bedroom to get a blue vial she kept in the desk by her bed, to pour a drop on both punctures, and then to wrap my hand in the fabric kept next to the vial in the drawer.

I thought it was a little strange she knew there were only two marks, but I did as I was told.

The stuff smelled awful. It burned my nose, along with my hand as I dripped it on. I wrapped my hand in the strange fabric as she had told me to do, and looked around the room.

It was in pristine condition, just like the rest of the house … no surprise there. What was surprising, though, were the four locks on the inside of the door. As I walked out of the room, I noticed scratch marks on the outside, like an animal had been trying to get in. Running my fingers across them, I noticed they were deep into the wood.

I shut the door behind me, deciding it was time to check on Margaret.

I tapped on her bedroom door and received no answer.

It was then I remembered Margaret needed her "after lunch snack" and figured she was down in the kitchen, waiting.

As I approached the kitchen, I saw Margaret crouching on the counter, bent over my purse. Smelling it.

I slowly approached her, and when she looked up, she had wild, inhuman eyes. The little girl I met earlier was no longer the girl that was in front of me. She pointed to the fridge and violently screamed at me to open it.

As I grabbed the snack package, she snatched it out of my hands and bellowed at me to leave.

She didn't need to tell me twice. I ran out of the kitchen, locked the door, and called her parents. They told me they would leave and come straight home.

The second I unlocked the kitchen door Margaret ran out giggling. She told me she had a fun day as she hugged my leg. Confused as shit, I grabbed my purse and decided to wait by the door for her parents to get home.

When they arrived, I told them I was sorry and that I didn't think I was going to be a good fit.

They told me they understood through hopeless and exhausted eyes, paid me for the day, and walked me to the door.

As I was walking out, they asked me to return Margaret's schedule. I handed it to them and asked what the knocking was. They told me it wasn't my concern and slammed the door in my face.

Walking back to my car, I looked up at the window to Margaret's room. She was looking down at me with the most sinister smile….

I got in my car and never returned.

To this day I wish I had taken a picture of the instructions to look back on later, but I was so freaked out at the time. I'm still not sure what they were feeding her, or why she was night and day around mealtime, or why she bit me, or what that knocking was.

I'm starting to wonder if *half-child* was a literal term instead of a typo, and that she was, in fact, half *something else*.

part three

The Wright Family

OUT OF ALL THE NANNY JOBS I HAVE taken, this particular one still haunts me, yet, comforts me at the same time.

I was hired by the Wright family a few years after my run in with the Johnsons. By then, the fear of any strange happenings had faded to the back of my mind, so I didn't hesitate to accept a position when they offered it.

They were a family of five, with three little kids; Bridget, Michael, and Sophia. Bridget was the eldest at nine, Michael was six, and little Sophia was four.

Their house was fairly small, but located on a good sized piece of land that even had a creek running through it. That's honestly why it was one of my favorite jobs: the creek was just so peaceful.

And the kids were great! They listened, they were exceptionally polite, and we always had a fun time together. There was just one thing I couldn't seem to get my mind off of: *the cup.*

They had placed this enormous yellow cup on top of their refrigerator. It was known as "Amelia's Cup". They told me that whenever something would go missing Amelia had taken it, and that the item would appear in the cup when it was needed by its owner.

At first I chalked this up to the kid's active imaginations. Their parents were most likely feeding into it, finding lost things to make a game of it.

I soon found this was not the case.

One day, while the kiddos were eating lunch and I was cleaning up the kitchen, I couldn't find the dish sponge. I searched everywhere and the kids got a good giggle out of my pantomime of "Where did the sponge go".

Finally, Bridget spoke up and said, "Check Amelia's cup."

I decided to play along, so I reached up inside of the cup. Sure enough, there was the sponge. I looked to Bridget and gave her a half smile, figuring she had hidden it up there as a joke. Kids can be so silly sometimes.

After lunch, we went to play outside by the creek. Michael and Bridget were kicking around a ball while little Sophia was skipping rocks. I walked over to Soph, who seemed to be having a conversation with someone, and knelt down beside her.

She turned to me and said, "Amelia wants you to know that she's sorry for borrowing the sponge. She had to soak up the water I spilled during lunch that I didn't tell you about. She said she didn't want any of us to slip, break our necks, and die."

Chilled goosebumps broke on my arms. That was a pretty graphic scenario for a four-year-old to think up. She must have picked it up from a movie she shouldn't have watched and was trying to be dramatic.

This pattern went on for a few more weeks, though; things would disappear from the house and reappear in Amelia's cup—a hairbrush, a doll, some earrings—always random items, but items that were needed at the time, nonetheless.

Then one day I couldn't find my car keys. After looking around the house I decided to check Amelia's cup.

There they were.

As I was pulling them out, Bridget walked in the kitchen and said, "Amelia says you shouldn't drive your car right now. It's broken and you might get hurt."

Mr. Wright peeked around the corner and told me he would take a look.

Warily, I followed him out to my car as he looked it over. Nothing seemed to be broken, so we started it up and let it run for a few minutes.

It started smoking.

The engine had caught fire.

I ran inside, grabbed the fire extinguisher, and put it out in mere minutes, but the damage was done.

A tow truck came and took my car to a nearby shop, and Mr. Wright offered to take me home. While we were driving, I decided to ask him about the whole Amelia business, since it seemed like things were starting to escalate.

Had he known my car was smoking earlier and decided to play a trick on me? Did he get the kids in on it too? I couldn't stand it any longer.

"Why do you and Mrs. Wright encourage this game about Amelia? It's cute, but I think it's a little strange, and maybe not healthy for the kids," I blurted out after a too-awkward stretch of silence.

Mr. Wright stiffened in his seat. He looked towards me and solemnly asked, "What makes you think it's a game?"

Unsure on how to answer, and figuring he didn't want to divulge the secret, I let it go.

When I got home, I decided to do some research.

I typed the Wright's address into Google, but after an hour of searching I had come up with nothing but an odd story about a house fire that had happened back in the twenties. There was no mention of anyone dying, or even who owned had the house at the time, so I let it go for the time.

The next day, I decided we would have a little picnic for lunch. As I was preparing the food, I heard Michael scream from outside.

"Oh no! A bee bit me!"

Bridget chimed in at the same moment, telling me that Michael was really allergic to bees. She said he had to go to the doctor last time it happened.

I scooped him up and brought him inside, set him on the couch and asked Bridget if he had an EpiPen somewhere. He did, but we couldn't find it.

Michael started to lose consciousness and I started to panic.

In a last-ditch effort, I reached into the cup and there it was; his EpiPen!

Once I had administered the epinephrine and knew Michael was okay, I called Mr. and Mrs. Wright to explain what had happened and assure them that everything was fine. They said they would be home immediately.

Sleepy Michael got tucked in on the couch and we all watched some TV until their parents arrived.

After that day, I always took the kids at their word when they told me things Amelia had said.

Most of the time it was really helpful.

One evening, we were all sitting around the kitchen table playing cards when there was a knock at the door. Mr. and Mrs. Wright were out for the night, so I knew it couldn't be them. Maybe it was a neighbor?

I walked over and nervously peeked through the peephole only to find the porch empty.

Must have been the wind, I thought to myself.

Just then, another knock came from the other side of the house.

I yelled for the kids to go up to Bridget's room, shut the door, and wait for me. I had a bad feeling about all of this.

As I made my way to the back door, I noticed the window next to it was open. A window I knew I had shut earlier in the day. Looking down, I saw muddy footprints leading out of the den. Panic rose in my chest as I heard a commotion coming from the kitchen.

As quietly as I could, and shaking with every step, I made my way towards the noise.

As I peered around the corner, I saw a man. He was rifling through all of the drawers and seemed to be looking for something.

I grabbed the closest thing to me, which happened to be an umbrella, and inched myself into view.

As soon as the man noticed my presence, he lunged.

Everything happened so quickly.

He grabbed a hold of me and I struggled to break free, but he had me pinned, knife to my throat, and pure venom in his eyes. His breath smelled of alcohol, cigarettes, and bad decisions.

Before I even had the chance to beg for my life, I heard a blood curdling scream coming from behind him. Startled, the intruder turned around just in time for Amelia's cup smash into his face with a loud *crunch*.

This gave me the opportunity I needed to wiggle free and bash him over the head with the umbrella. Obviously, it didn't do much damage, but the cup had. He was holding his face as blood poured from his forehead and nose, and scrambling towards the door.

As he ran out, I called the police and booked it up the stairs to the children. We locked ourselves in Bridget's closet.

I held them all until help arrived.

Within twenty minutes, the house was flooded with police, and Mr. and Mrs. Wright had come home.

The police asked us all a long list of questions and took down my account of the. Thankfully, the kids knew nothing of the situation other than having been bored in Bridget's room.

As the police picked up evidence, one officer asked Mr. Wright why they kept a cup full of bricks in the house. Mrs. Wright looked over at me, quickly shaking her head before her husband answered.

Mr. Wright gave some hogwash excuse as to why they were there, and the officer let it go.

The police left. Mr. and Mrs. Wright tucked the kids into bed and profusely thanked me for saving their children's lives.

We all know, it wasn't me though.

I stayed with the Wrights as their nanny for about a year. Amelia was always part of the daily routine. After everything that had happened and the close calls that she had prevented, I guess I was okay with that.

The Chicubari

In Australia, you always hear that animals should be your biggest fear. While that may be true, those people probably haven't heard of the Chicubari.

I was in my first year of med school and wanted to travel the world in search of new horizons, so I decided to take a break and explore. I had been dealt some shit rolls in life, especially at the time, and needed something new to clear my head. I needed to be somewhere I could feel free.

I decided to travel to Queensland, Australia, with four of my closest friends: Bridget, Todd, Michael, and Sidney. We were all searching for the same thing: adventure.

"Hey, thanks again for the invite, Ganeia. This is going to be awesome," Todd said as he took his place on the plane. The rest of my friends nodded in agreement.

Full of excitement upon arrival, we booked our first tour into the Australian outback. Our guide was a short little Aussie man named Blake. He had a big, bushy beard and a strong accent—one you would imagine every Australian has.

We all hopped into his car and headed out on an adventure that would soon change our lives.

It took us about three hours to get where we were going, which apparently was an Australian rainforest known as "Gondwana".

As we got out of the car, an unsettling hush fell across the forest. The birds had stopped singing; the wind had stopped whistling—complete silence enveloped everything. As we approached the opening to the trail, a weird feeling settled over me.

This place felt … wrong.

I trudged forward with my enthusiastic group as they commented on the scenery before us. I'll admit, it was beautiful and unlike anything we have in the States: truly breathtaking.

I slowed to catch my breath, trying to shake the anxiety that was becoming increasingly worse the deeper we went.

We soon approached a statue. Blake knelt down beside it and laid out what looked to be a handmade doll. The others seemed to be off in their own worlds as I approached him.

"What is that for?" I asked nervously.

"The Chicubari," he whispered as he handed one of the strange dolls to me and watched me with his piercing eyes.

I shuddered, placing the doll next to his.

Before I could ask him further questions, though, Bridget shouted that she'd seen a kangaroo and took off into the trees. Blake fell back onto his heels as he shot up from his crouch, tossing the other four dolls from his hands as Sid, Michael, and Todd raced off into the forest after Bridget, leaving Blake and me behind.

Blake shot a worried glance at me, but before he could explain, we heard the screams.

Our guide booked it the fuck out of there and left me. Not that I blamed him—I was terrified too, but I couldn't just leave my friends behind.

I turned towards the screams and decided to follow the path I thought they had taken.

As I walked the trail, I felt the air get noticeably colder, even though it was midday and should easily still have been about eighty degrees. I pulled on my jacket and continued on for what felt like hours before I finally came to a clearing.

Before me was the most horrifying scene I had ever witnessed in my entire twenty-two years of life.

All four of my friends were tied to branches that had been shaped into Xs around a circle of stones. Each of them had a strange design cut into their stomachs and fresh blood dripped down their sides.

I quickly ran to Bridget—she was closest to me. As I tugged on her leg, trying to figure out how to free her, she let out a soft groan. Nothing else. And her eyes were trained on the circle of rocks, almost as if they were being forced there.

I moved to Sidney next, but she was in the same state. They all were.

Panicking, I started to cut the rope that held them to the branches in hopes of freeing them. Just as I got Michael's right hand free, I heard an ear-piercing howl from just beyond the tree line. My friends began shaking as tears stained their cheeks. I turned towards the sound just in time to see a flash of what appeared to be a man, but only barely.

The creature stood on impossibly long legs that were bent in an inhuman way. It was thin and bony with strange markings carved deep into its skin (I recognized one symbol as it had also been carved into my best friend's abdomen) and its face was black with decaying flesh melting from its bones.

I tried to run, but I was paralyzed by fear.

Its blood red eyes locked onto mine.

The creature began to shake, turning its head from side to side as a thin smile formed on its face. The smile spread as its cheeks grew bigger and bigger, revealing rows of sharp, bloodstained teeth.

I watched in horror as it began to stalk towards me, like a lion about to devour its prey. It wove its way in and out of the brush, almost dancing. As it came closer, I could smell it, the putrid stench of rotting flesh mixed with sour milk.

I instinctively threw my hand over my mouth, gagging on the smells, when the zombie-like creature jolted towards me.

It reached out as it started to vibrate in place and I suddenly felt dizzy. My vision blurred, and before I knew it, it was stroking my face and it—it smelled me.

The creature clicked its teeth together— a sound which quickly became more like chomping—and then rammed its bony finger into my forehead.

I screamed out in agony as I felt all of the pain the creature had endured in its infinite lifetime crash down on me all at once. I saw death and despair as a heavy darkness washed over me, isolating in my own personal hell. My mouth was dry and I felt the life being sucked out of me; the creature was feeding on my fear and my pain. It needed it. This was how it survived.

This agony lasted for what could have been forever, but eventually it stopped. I fell to the ground and wrapped my arms around my trembling body, sobbing uncontrollably.

I saw the creature standing above me, and then it turned. I fell on my hands, reaching for it, as I knew what was coming next.

I shakily climbed to my feet and watched in horror as he began vibrating again, placing a finger on each of my friends' foreheads. I watched the fear on their faces twist into agony, the life slowly draining from each of their eyes as the Chicubari fed off of them. They soon became nothing but soulless vessels, but it didn't stop there.

The monster's eyes changed from red to black as hundreds of spiders crawled out of the dark spaces and marched towards my friends' bodies. They made their way up the posts, stopping once they reached the top. Thousands of tiny eyes looked to their master for approval before one by one crawling into my friends' ears.

My friends began to shake violently from the intruders, and then ... nothing.

I fell to my knees again, more tears streaming down my already raw cheeks. The creature stared at me with what looked to be almost heartbreak in its eyes, and with that, it bolted back towards the tree line.

I sat there for a long while beneath what used to be my friends, staring just beyond the trees in search of the Chicubari, but it was long gone. I was left empty and alone, wishing it would have taken me too.

The clearing was blanketed by a deafening silence as I slowly picked myself up from the ground. As I turned to leave, I heard the sound of teeth chomping in the air. I froze and slowly glanced behind me. A new wave of terror rushed over my body as I watched each of my friends' eyes jerk open.

All at once their heads jolted in my direction, eyes glazed over and raw. I stumbled backwards as I watched spiders crawl out of their mouths, some getting crushed by their chomping teeth along the way.

They stopped chomping once they hit the ground, and together they all turned towards me.

I ran out of there as fast as I could, heading back towards the statue and the edge of the rainforest. I was just about to pass it when I remembered the four dolls that had been tossed down by our guide, and a thought occurred to me.

I quickly picked them up, shoving them next to my own, and waited.

Silence.

I slowly crept back to the clearing where I'd left my friends, my heart beating like a drum in my chest the whole way. Once I reached the tree line, I stopped.

The clearing was empty.

No posts, no friends, no spiders, and no Chicubari.

Confused, I left the forest and quickly made my way back to our hotel to pack my bags and get the hell out of that God forsaken country. When I arrived, I found that my friend's belongings had disappeared. It was as if they had never existed, but I knew what they had become.

I got on the next plane back to America and never spoke of them again, until now. I need to warn all other thrill seekers like myself about what could await you in Australia. As if it needed *more* things that could kill you.

I learned a lot from the Chicubari that touched me. Its pain wasn't the only thing it gave me. It also gave me nightmares that tell me its story, over and over again.

That's how I know the Chicubari are what is left over from tortured souls. They prey on the weak, working their way into their minds and taking their will to live. No man or beast can resist them once they have been marked.

So, if you are going to Queensland, Australia, make sure you place an offering before you enter the Gondwana rainforest, or it will be your life that is offered in its place.

My friends will make sure of it.

The Cemetery

Most of my childhood was spent exploring the cemetery next to my house. I know, weird, right? Well, to an eight-year-old, it was anything but. I remember passing by each gravestone, saying each name out loud as I imagined what their lives must have been like. Take John Wilcox for instance; I always imagined he was a doctor who lost one too many patients, tragically ridden with guilt, resulting in a gruesome suicide. Maybe he even killed his family first—I had a very active imagination.

I remember the day I met Susan. I had left my house early in the morning, giving my mother a quick kiss on the cheek, as I grabbed the sack lunch I had prepared. I was making my way to the back entrance of the cemetery, when I saw a girl sitting next to a grave in the far corner. I froze, not used to having my morning adventures disturbed. Why was she there? Was she crying?

Being curious, I slowly walked towards her, trying to get a discreet look at the name on the gravestone. I must have stepped on a branch because the girl turned around quickly, wiping tears from her eyes as she did.

"H—hi," she said shyly.

I bent down next to her and I could see the name, Susanna Bryant. The girl turned her head back towards the grave, letting out a long sigh before saying, "I miss my mom so much." My heart breaking for her, I reached out and touched her shoulder, letting her know I was sorry. She looked over at me with a slight smile and told me her name was Susan—and just like that, we were friends.

Susan and I were so much alike, except for the fact that she was never cold, and she didn't like wearing shoes—so strange. The day we met, I had asked her to come over for dinner at my place, excited to have a new friend, but she sadly replied she couldn't. It was okay though; we shared my sack lunch instead!

When evening came, I told Susan I had to go home, but would see her again tomorrow. She looked a little sad as she watched me leave, but I thought to myself that I would make her a friendship bracelet when I got home, that would make her happy! I walked into my house and made my way up to my room to start on it, dinner could wait! I grabbed my beads off my dresser and went into my favorite little space in my closet where I would work on it the rest of the night.

The next day, Susan was already at the cemetery when I got there. She greeted me with a curious smile as I pulled out the bracelet. Her face lit up. Again, she wasn't wearing shoes or a coat. "Aren't you freezing?" I asked, as I tied the bracelet around her wrist. She changed the subject and began talking about how pretty her new bracelet was and how we were going to be best friends forever—oh, to be young again.

We walked around for a few hours before my stomach started to growl, I hadn't eaten since lunch yesterday and was famished! I begged my new friend to come over to my place for lunch and told her my mom would make us something really yummy! She seemed a little worried, but eventually said okay, I was excited!

We made our way out the back gate and across the street to my place. I excitedly walked up my steps and opened the door for Susan who was shyly walking behind me. As we walked in and made our way to the kitchen, I heard her gasp. I turned around to see why, but before I could say anything, she was running out of my house.

Confused, I turned towards my mom who was sitting at the kitchen table. She had her mouth open like she was going to talk but didn't quite have the words. I stood there for a minute, waiting for her to comfort me, but it never happened. Feeling hurt, I sighed and sulked off to my room, completely forgetting about the fact I was starving.

Two hours later there was a knock on my door. I excitedly ran down the stairs thinking it was Susan. Maybe she was just concerned that her dad didn't know where she was. Maybe she had to go tell him first. I threw open the door, but instead of Susan standing there, there was a policeman in her place. I looked behind him and saw Susan and what I assumed to be her dad in the street, she was crying as he hugged her.

The next thing I know, I'm being placed in the back of a police car. More police officers arrived, along with paramedics. I sat in the back of the cruiser confused, why were my parents letting this happen? A lady in a nice suit suddenly approached me and pulled me out of the car. She sat me down and began asking me all kinds of questions. My ears started to ring as I felt a lump form in the back of my throat, fighting back tears, I remembered.

THE CEMETERY

I remembered the night my father came home, drunk and belligerent. He began yelling at my mother. My older brother Jake told me to go up to my room and moments later I heard the gunshots. I hid in my closet, clutching my teddy bear as tears ran down my face. I heard my brother yell something as two more shots rang through the house. I listened closely; someone was coming up the stairs.

I heard my father mumble something, was he saying sorry? He was crying. That's when I heard one more shot, and then silence. I fell asleep that night in my closet, too terrified to leave.

That was twelve years ago. My therapist says that when someone goes through something as traumatic as I did, it's normal to block it out and continue on as if things were normal. A coping mechanism I suppose. To this day though, I will never understand why Susan never wore shoes.

Six Minutes

I'M NOT SURE HOW LONG I HAVE BEEN trapped down here; weeks, months, a year? Time has blended together, and I fear it is coming to an end. I woke up this morning in my usual state; chained to a desk with a typewriter in front of me. I never know how I get here; I'm guessing they drug my water each day and place me in this chair before I wake, but who really knows.

There has been a timer sitting next to me every day, and once the alarm sounds, it starts it's count down. At first, I wasn't sure what it meant, all I knew was that when it ended, it meant pain was coming—severe pain. Strangers in black masks would come barging in with bats, knives, and piggy prods, beating me to no end until I passed out. Over and over again, every day the same, until I figured out what they expected of me.

The first day I typed a continuation to a story I had long forgotten about, was the first day they brought me food instead of beatings. With a newfound will to live I made sure I typed a chapter every day, sometimes two, and everyday food would come. It wasn't much really, some toast, some water, maybe a power bar, but it was enough to keep me going.

I'm guessing some days my captor wouldn't approve of what I wrote, because on those days I received beatings with my food, how fun is that?

I finished the book yesterday, barely. I've lost so much blood, and I can barely see out of my eyes due to the swelling. I have 6 broken fingers which has made typing almost unbearable, and my ankle is dislocated. I have lost so much blood; I don't know how I am even alive.

When I woke up this morning, I half expected to be released, but something is wrong. I was still chained to this miserable chair, typewriter taunting me from its usual place, and that damn timer slowly counting down. I have no idea what they expect from me this time, and one more beating will certainly be my last.

I had six minutes. Six minutes until this was all over. Six minutes to write this down in hopes that someone, someday, would find it. I had six minutes, and now I have none.

Gracie

*I*F THERE IS ONE THING EVERYONE knows about me: it's my fear of dolls. I *hate* them. Their soulless eyes and cheeky, psychopathic smiles are enough to send me into a full panic attack at moment's notice. My parents always thought my fear was irrational, given the fact that I personally used to own a lot of them. A traumatic memory that has long been forgotten, obviously.

Now, my niece loves dolls. She even collects them, placing them in glass cases around her room. A room I never enter when I visit. My sister always yells at me when I come over, she doesn't want my fear to rub off on Bailey. "You are 26 years old, Sarah, time to grow up," she would say. But I will never grow out of this fear.

Last night my sister called and asked if I could watch Bailey, as she had some hot date with a *dreamy* lawyer. I teased her about it before saying yes, I really didn't have anything else to do that night, anyways.

I pulled up to her house later that evening and was greeted by an enthusiastic Bailey. "Sarah! Guess what? Momma gave me your old dolls!" I wrapped my arms around my excited niece and glared up at my sister who was standing in the doorway, with an apologetic look on her face. As I approached, she shrugged at me. "What? You weren't using them anymore and mom thought they needed some love."

I shook my head with disgust and walked through the door, purposely giving her a shove as I went. Bailey was jumping up and down, pigtails bouncing in the air. "Do you want to see them? I know Gracie has been asking about you, she says she misses you," my little niece looked up at me with hopeful eyes. I shuddered, but before I could reply, I felt my sister shooting daggers into the back of my head.

I peeked over my shoulder, and grimaced. "Uh, sure Bailey. I'd, uh, love to…" I choked out. My sister smiled and grabbed her coat. "You two have fun,"

GRACIE

she chided, before heading out the door to her car. I let out a dramatic sigh as Bailey grabbed my hand, leading me to her room.

I began to feel nauseous as she opened the door. *Stop it Sarah, you are going to scare Bailey*, my sister's remarks flooded into my mind. I gulped and followed her in.

The room was just as horrible as I imagined. Beady little eyes stared at me from every angle, and I shuddered as I closed mine. Bailey began tugging at me. "Look aunty, remember her?" I slowly opened my eyes to my niece shoving an old porcelain doll into my face.

Oh, I remembered her. The doll had hair as black as her soul with eyes that seemed to lock onto mine, as Bailey bounced her excitedly in front of me. Her never ending smile was the one that haunted my dreams, sending shivers throughout my whole body. She was terrifying, had this really been my favorite doll?

Bailey placed her in my hands. She was as cold and limp as a lifeless child, and yet, as alive in my mind as any lurking creature—wishing to carefully feast upon every last inch of my fears. I was frozen in place, fear had started to take over my whole body, when Bailey finally took the demon doll back—breaking the petrifying trance I was in.

I looked down at my niece who was now stroking Gracie's hair lovingly, "I want to play hide and seek," she said.

Perfect! I thought, as I walked towards the door. "I want Gracie to play too," my niece called out, before I could reach the safety of the hallway. "Ugh, why?" I replied under my breath, not wanting to upset her.

"We'll hide first!" She excitedly announced, as she ran past me, Gracie in tow. "Start counting!"

When I had walked far enough away from the room of nightmares, I began to count. When I had reached 30, I called out, "ready or not, here I come!" I heard a giggle coming from the coat closet, but pretended to look everywhere else, before announcing I had found her.

The game went on for an hour before I remembered it was well past Bailey's bedtime. I found her one last time before telling her as much. Bailey did her normal, "I'm not sleepy" tirade, before looking at me with a horrified expression. "Did you find Gracie?"

I looked at her confused. "What do you mean? I thought you two hid together?"

My niece yawned. "No, she wanted you to find her yourself, you have to Sarah," she sleepily replied.

I rolled my eyes and told her I would look for her after she went to bed. My niece seemed to accept my answer and bounded towards her room, but not before she shot back, "Gracie said, if you don't find her, she will find you!"

A shiver ran down my back, like tiny little spiders crawling along my spine, causing goosebumps to rise all over my body. I made my way to the kitchen, pulling out a pint of ice-cream. I decided I would eat away my fears, while simultaneously indulging in some trash TV. Two hours passed before I heard my sister's car pull into the driveway.

When she walked in, I told her about my horrible night and how Bailey had really freaked me out with her dolls. I also sarcastically mentioned that she had hidden Gracie somewhere in the house, winking at her, as I opened the door to leave. I laughed a little, thinking about my sister finding her in her bed or something, scaring the crap out of her.

As I drove back to my apartment, I began thinking about all the nightmares I was going to endure that night. I blasted some Lindsey Sterling, trying to ease my fear. As I parked my car, a thought crossed my mind and I reflexively looked into the back seat. It was empty. I sighed and got out of the car, almost mad at myself for letting this shit get to me.

As I approached my apartment, I stopped. My door was open ajar, with the inside of my place encased by darkness. Taped upon it, was a folded-up piece of paper. I reached for the note, slowly opening it with my heart racing in my chest. A lump immediately formed in the back of my throat as I read it out loud, tears filling my eyes. Three little words, written with an elegant hand, that would haunt me for the rest of my life.

I found you.

Someone is Stealing My Stories

As WRITERS, WE ALL HAVE OUR OWN inspirations—mine come from my journal. After every victim, I record my adventure in impeccable detail; how it happened, what I felt, the look they gave me. You know, real life horror makes the best stories and my readers deserve the best!

I was really excited about my last conquest, boy, was he a gusher—I had taken my time with this one, enjoyed every horrifying moment. I peered over at the journal on my nightstand. One last read before bed:

Male. 22. Red hair, green eyes, perfect freckled body. No cameras. Long private drive. Owns a small dog.

Routine:

(5:45 a.m.) School at [redacted].
(10:00 a.m.) Work at [redacted] Diner.
(2:00 p.m.) Not-so-secret smoke break.
(6:00 p.m.) Heads home to [redacted], house number [redacted].
(7:30 p.m.) Opens bottle of wine, usually red.
(8:30 p.m.) Forgets to check the locks before snuggling into bed. Stupid boy.

I decided the best time to grab him was 6:30, right outside of his car, and he never saw it coming. I placed the chloroform-soaked rag over his mouth discreetly and out he went, thank God he was the same height as me or this could have been difficult. Once he was loaded in my van, I drove to my cabin. Loaded. Locked. Ready to begin as adrenaline coursed through my veins.

I wanted him awake. I wanted to watch the life slowly drain from his emerald eyes as I began my egregious ritual. I started with his achilleas, not having that mistake again, my body is far too old for a cat and mouse chase these days.

I drove the blade into each tendon with a precision of a surgeon as he slashed against the restraints. That was enough of that, pop goes the spine. Ah, much better.

From there, I stabbed each pressure point to ensure the most pain. He was a gusher and it gave me joy. I had placed a bucket on each side of his head to catch his tears, as they would make a killer energy drink later.

I moved onto each appendage, making sure to stab the knife under every nail before methodically breaking each one with a gentle snap. I shivered with excitement as I slowly traced alongside his pulsing wrists, avoiding the main arteries.

When I was done with my slicing and dicing, I bent down and whispered in his ear. "Don't worry, you will live!" His eyes grew wide with a twinkle of hope for the first time since he had awakened. That's when I took my knife and stabbed down hard, straight into his heart, the look of betrayal scratching my deep itch as her life faded.

I heard an owl in the distance as I looked at my craftsmanship with the utmost admiration. Pleased with my finished product, I loaded him up in my van, and buried him in his backyard.

Side note: make sure to mention Poppy the pooch in story. She quite enjoyed the fingers I left for her. Can't have her starving in her owner's absence: I'm not a monster.

I set my journal back down, giving it a small pat of approval and drifted off to sleep. The itch had been scratched. For now.

Around 8:00 a.m., I woke up feeling energized and ready to write. My dreams had given me more than I had hoped for in terms of inspiration. I reached for my morning cup of tears and my journal, excitedly opening it up to the bookmarked page.

My blood ran cold.

My entry was gone and in its place was a quickly jotted down note that read, "thanks for this, I'd say it's your best work yet, can't wait to write about it."

I immediately ran downstairs to check my surveillance cameras. As the feed loaded up onto my computer, I hit the rewind function to view the footage, but I only made it to the last hour before I hit play.

I watched as someone, something, came into my home. It was raw, like a baby. Slick and pink as it crept around my house. It resembled a human, but only—wrong. The things face kept switching. First it looked like a girl, with long blonde hair. Then, a boy with a buzz cut.

The scariest part was when it entered my bedroom. My sanctuary. It stole my journal from my nightstand, quickly scribbled the note and then gingerly, kissed me on the forehead.

I reached up to touch where it had planted the kiss and felt a thin layer of film. I shivered in disgust. My eyes glanced back to the screen and I watched myself wake up just as the being slithered out of my room. I watched it walk down the hallway minutes before I had hopped up from my bed. It must have heard me, because it quickly ducked into my coat closet.

My heart began to race as I turned to the door behind me—it was ajar.

Holding my breath, I quietly got up from the chair and made my way to the closet, luckily passing my knife block on the way. I grabbed the biggest, sharpest one I could find and reached for the knob.

It was empty.

I released the breath I had been holding and slammed the door shut! As I made my way back to my computer, I looked to my left and noticed the window above my kitchen sink was open. I immediately ran to my computer and hit play, already knowing what I would find.

The thief snuck out of the closet the minute I had turned on the surveillance feed. I watched as he, it, climbed through the kitchen window like a slippery eel. My story, still in its pocket.

I don't know why this multi-faced creature wants my stories, but I just saw another author write about them, and it seems I'm not the only one who's encounter this thing. I don't think I'll be the last.

Daydreams

*H*AVE YOU EVER STARTED DAYDREAMING
and after a while start wondering how your brain actually creates these random scenarios?

This morning I was sitting at the kitchen table, slowly shoveling some Cinnamon Toast Crunch into my face as I stared blankly out the window. I was always the first one to wake and it was in these brief moments that I did my best thinking. I watched a distant crow peck the ground as I thought about that saying, "the early bird gets the worm."

Worms, slimy little dirt creatures.

I wonder what else lives underground with them.

I sat there for a moment picturing other bugs using worms as transportation in some kind of underground world, when another thought crossed my mind. Just briefly, it was almost a flash, but I saw myself running through the woods in a panic with a boy by my side.

I knew he looked familiar but for some reason I couldn't place him. I sat there puzzled for a moment before returning to my cereal. As I looked down a name echoed in my head. Michael.

I was so lost in thought that I didn't hear my mother enter the kitchen.

"Good morning honey," her voice pulled me out of my trance.

"Oh, hey Mom. Morning. Hey uh, do I know a Michael?" I looked up at her just in time to see her face turn white.

She quickly turned her back to me, "Umm ... not that I can think of. Hey, you better get dressed, bus will be here soon." she quickly added before putting the coffee pot back and exiting the kitchen.

I sat there, brows creased for a few minutes, before I got up and walked to my room. My mom was obviously hiding something, and I was determined to find out what it was. As soon as I was dressed, I shouted a quick "see ya," to my mom and headed out the door.

School was about a mile away and most days I took the bus, but today I decided a good walk would help me sort through my thoughts. *Where was that forest? Who was that boy? Was he Michael?*

School went by terribly slow, per usual, until last period. Mr. Johnson was handing back our tests from last week when he stopped next to my desk, "great job Eric, I'm really impressed with how well you are adjusting," he looked down at me with a strange grin. I looked up at him confused as hell, "uh, thanks, I guess ..." was all I managed to get out before the bell rang.

I took the bus home, no longer wanting to be lost in thought. As I made my way to our porch, I noticed a strange car in the driveway. Who was here? I reached the top step and carefully opened the door as I slowly slipped into the house. I heard my mom shouting at someone from the kitchen, "No, I'm telling you he remembers!" My heart started to pound in my chest as I took a step back toward the front door.

Creak.

Damn these floorboards. I looked up in time to see a man swiftly coming towards me, but before I had the chance to even begin to process what was happening, the world went dark.

When I woke up, I was in an office of some sort. I struggled to gain my focus enough to try and get an idea of exactly where I was, when I noticed I was tied

DAYDREAMS

to a chair. I started to panic! Where was my mother? Why was I here? My eyes started to swell with tears when I heard a light tap.

"Eric, is that you?" A small whisper came from behind the door to my right.

"Ye—yeah?" I cautiously replied. "Who are you? Do you know why I'm here?"

There was a heavy sigh on the other side of the door and the boy replied, "no one man, I'm no one." Suddenly, a picture slid under the frame. I stretched my neck as far as I could to see what it was when I heard the word, *"Sveglio."*

Memories came flooding back. I remembered the day my brother Michael and I tried to leave the farm. I remembered how scared we were as we scaled the last fence blocking our freedom. We made it about ten yards before they shot Michael. He begged for me to keep going as he hit the ground in agony, but I couldn't leave him.

I held my brother in my arms as he took his last breath, praying to anyone that would listen to not take him from me, but no one cared. When the guards got to me, I was just a pile of broken hope, there's nothing else they could do to me that would feel worse than this, or so I thought.

My punishment? Well, my punishment was to dispose of Michael's body. Piece by piece, pie by pie.

Boys must eat after all, but not me, I would starve for the next three days. Starve in the hell hole built upon fear shaped tears, extracted from stolen boys with broken dreams.

With tears running down my cheeks I looked down at the photo of Michael lying beside me. I had to get out of here. I started pulling on my restraints causing my wrists to bleed enough to slip through. I rushed to the door and quickly dashed out; no time to be cautious. I passed by the dark room—something we all called it because that's all you remember when you come out; darkness.

That is, if you are lucky enough to come out. Sometimes there would be screams for hours upon hours. We would all clutch our pillows to our ears trying to drown out the sounds. None of us knew what caused someone to scream like that, because when we had the chance to find out, we never remembered—probably for the best.

I kept running. Shaking images of cold, steel-like rods out of my mind as I rubbed my temples. I turned another corner and the front door was finally in view. So close, so close!

Darkness.

When I opened my eyes, I was sitting at my kitchen table, half eaten bowl of Cinnamon Toast

Crunch rested in front of me. My mom came into the kitchen, "Good morning honey! How did you sleep?"

***

Do you ever start daydreaming, and after a while start to wonder if maybe those dreams are really memories?

Well, they just might be.

The BEK

THREE YEARS AGO, BRAD AND I MOVED to an apartment in a secluded little town called Lakeland. We chose this town because it was peaceful, a good neighborhood, and just an all-around relaxing energy; much needed due to the fact that my husband worked nights and I wanted to feel safe when I was alone.

We moved in quickly, made our new place a home and even though I hated stairs with every part of my being, we chose the top floor of the complex because "who would climb four sets of stairs to harass someone?"

A couple weeks went by and once we were completely settled, I reached out to my neighbors across the way. Even going as far as bringing them a plate of cookies as a friendly gesture. It was a young couple, James and Evie, really nice people. James was a welder and Evie was a nurse, and since they had opposite schedules I would always have someone across the way, which made me feel even safer!

Everything was perfect; I was loving our new home and neighbors and finally felt at peace. Late one night while I was catching up on The Flash, I heard a knock at the door. I looked at the clock and it was 11:00 p.m., who would be knocking on our door at this hour? I made my way to the sound and looked through our peephole only to realize the knock hadn't come from our door, it came from our neighbor's.

Outside their stoop were two young kids, they looked to be about thirteen and maybe six. Confused, I just stood there watching them until I heard one ask to use our neighbor's phone. James was the one home as Evie worked night shift, but I didn't see him open his door at all or even respond.

At first this all just seemed odd, but really nothing too strange, maybe they were lost, and the other neighbors didn't answer their doors? It wasn't until they both looked over at me that I realized this situation was more than just odd. Did they know I was looking at them? How did they know I was there? I was sure I hadn't made a sound.

The way they looked at my door made me think they could see right through it. If that wasn't creepy enough, the more I focused on them I realized they had dark black eyes, as if their pupils were fully dilated or something. Then, all of a sudden, this feeling of complete dread rushed over me, it felt like death itself. My breath ran cold and the hair on the back of my neck stood on end. My stomach was tied in knots and it felt as if someone had knocked the wind right out of me. I immediately stepped away from the door, waiting for a knock, or for someone to call out to me.

After what felt like an eternity, I peeked through the peephole again and they were gone, along with the feeling of death. I returned to the couch and sat there with so many questions running through my mind. Why were these kids wandering around late at night, why did they climb up four flights of stairs to use a stranger's phone, and why did I feel so terrified of them?

The next morning, I ran into James on my way out for a grocery run, I couldn't help but ask him about the night before. He looked at me a little shaken, asked if they had come to my door too. I told him how I had watched the whole exchange but all they had done was look at my door.

When I asked him if he had let them use his phone, he said he hadn't because they looked like they were on drugs or something and that he just felt wrong about the whole situation. They showed no emotion and talked in a flat tone. He also told me how he called the police and they told him that him and his friends needed to stop calling in with the same story or they would be in trouble.

Fast forward to a couple months later. I was telling my friend about these strange children and she just kept staring at me in shock. She asked me if I had ever heard of "The Black-Eyed Children". I laughed and told her no. She typed it in on her phone and handed it to me and holy shitballs, there is a lot of people who have had the same experience.

From what I read, it's a good thing my neighbor didn't open his door. Apparently, if he would have, he could have died. Some people reported that their family members caught an illness after letting them in and dying a horrible slow death. There were also reports that they sometimes return to the houses they seek out, to finish what they started and that Lakeland itself had, had its fair share of encounters.

After all my research I no longer felt safe in our little community. I told Brad everything and he agreed that we could break our lease and move if it meant I would have a peace of mind. We packed up our things, said our goodbyes to James and Evie, and got the hell out of Lakeland.

It's been one year, and we have moved into a townhome in an even more secluded area. The first month we moved in I kept feeling like someone was watching me late at night. Brad decided we would adopt a dog to keep me company and maybe make me feel a little at ease. When we walked into the humane society and I saw this big fluffy German Shepherd type dog named Murdock, I knew he was the perfect fit, I called him my little Dare Devil. We eventually started to settle in. Having Murdock to keep me company at night was the best decision we could have made, but then the knocking started.

Someone would knock on our door almost every other night. Just three solid knocks. *Knock, knock, knock.* Murdock would go crazy but when I tried to see who it was, there was never anyone there. This continued for a whole month, it was only at night, only at 11:00 p.m., and only when I was by myself with Murdock. Sometimes I would hear giggling. Not your average kid playing a prank giggles though, no, it was a sound that sent shivers through my bones and made me want to vomit.

Brad started to suggest I talk to someone and that maybe stress had gotten the better of me, I knew better though. Then, one night as I was cleaning off dinner dishes, (Brad actually had the night off) we heard one big bang. He ran to the door and swung it open so fast, but as I had already anticipated, no one there. We never heard any knocks after that but I still get the feeling I'm being watched from time to time.

We aren't sure if it was neighbor kids playing a prank, or if the creepy black-eyed children had followed us, but either way, I won't be opening my door to strange knocks at night and neither should you.

The Price of a Soul

ABOUT A MONTH AGO, I RECEIVED A friend request on Facebook from an old High School acquaintance: Lacey Bradshaw.

Now, we all know what that means, within five to ten minutes I would most likely receive a sales pitch about whatever MLM company she was a part of and how I would be the perfect fit.

Feeling bored and in need of some amusement I accepted the request and waited.

Surprise, surprise, within five minutes I heard the familiar "ding" that would sound when I had received a message. Amused, I opened it and sure enough it was a sales pitch.

> *"Hey Tiffany, it's been soooooo long! We should definitely catch up soon. How has life*

been? Anything new? My life has been pretty great actually and I thought I would share with you why! I recently found this new company called "Soul Refresher", it's not like your everyday company that sells leggings, over-priced makeup or bath bombs, it's a company that actually helps people learn to relax and meditate and find their way in the world! A soul refresher! If you want to learn more, shoot me a message! Kisses xoxo"

A little intrigued, I messaged Lacey back and asked for more info; after all, I wasn't doing much with my life and this sounded interesting.

Once again, she responded and told me more about the company. Apparently, they sold books, but when I looked up reviews, I was shocked! Almost every single review out of thousands had given the company five stars and said it truly helped them turn their life around.

Lacey told me if I signed up under her it would be half off a normal joining fee and that she would teach me everything I needed to know.

I didn't really have much to lose so I said sure, and upon paying the $50 signing fee I was sent everything I needed to start my journey into this business.

Selling was fairly easy; everyone could use a good ol' soul refresher and a break in their crazy hectic lives every now and then. I actually had sold five books to random acquaintances within a week of joining and I had made $100 off of those five sales.

Feeling pretty good I decided I should try to find people to sell under me, as Lacey was also making $10 off of every sale I made.

Now this is where things got weird, I received another message from Lacey asking me if I had actually read the book. I felt a little foolish once I realized I hadn't and when I told her as much, she became hostile and told me it was of the utmost importance that I read the book immediately. So, I did.

It really wasn't anything special, just your typical life coach advice and breathing techniques, real boring actually. When I finished reading, I realized I had lost track of time and it was dark out, I was sure it had only been lunch time when I started.

Feeling sluggish and oddly exhausted I crawled into bed and fell asleep. The next day I received another message from Lacey thanking me for reading the book. I was a bit confused by the fact I hadn't yet told her I had read it but decided to brush it off and went back to my daily search of people willing to buy the book.

As the days went on, I realized I was feeling more and more tired, and just over all run down, it was hard to stay focused on selling when all I wanted to do was sleep. I wasn't even hungry. Sleep and sell, that was my life.

Eventually I found an acquaintance; Brooke, from my hip hop dance class back in the day who said she wanted to sell some books herself.

Ecstatic I sent her all the info she would need and repeated what Lacey had told me; that she should read the book upon receiving it so she had a better understanding of what she was pitching to people.

About two days later I received a huge signing bonus and also a message from Brooke telling me she had received her book and would start reading it that night.

After selling one more book to my neighbor across from me I crawled into bed for the fourth time that day and fell asleep.

When I woke up, I instantly realized I felt like a brand-new person. I rushed to the bathroom and realized I even looked younger, and maybe even slightly more in shape. I thought to myself wow; this book really does work!

A week or so went by and I got another strange message, this time from Brooke, she wasn't having trouble selling her books, but she was having a hard time getting anyone to sign up under her. She said she was feeling terrible and sluggish and had no motivation.

The strangest part was the worse that she felt, the better I did. I know that sounds horrible, but it was true, I had never felt better in my entire life. It's been five days now since I have heard from Brooke, which is no surprise considering I saw in the newspaper that she had passed away in her sleep, it's really quite sad, but on the plus side, I feel amazing!

A few days ago, I found two more people to sell under me and they seem to be doing quite well. Every book they sell not only do I get a percentage, but I also get an invigorating burst of energy and satisfaction that I have never felt before.

Soul Refresher has been a miracle for my life and I'm sure has added years to it. With that being said, would anyone love to hear more about this amazing company and possibly sell some books?

It's to die for.

Forgotten Thoughts

---

*E*VERYONE WILL STOP LOOKING FOR

the monsters under their bed, when they realize the true monsters are inside of their head.

Have any of you ever walked into a room and forgotten why? I have on many occasions. I always feel like there is a reason, but I just can't place my finger on it. *Was I going to brush my teeth? Was I going to grab a book?* I'll retrace my thoughts back to the moments before, but usually come up blank. Sometimes I remember later that day, while other times the thought never resurfaces—bugging me to no end. *What did I need?*

Everyone has experienced this at some point in their life. Most of time it's because we are so lost in thought—thinking of something when another thought pops up simultaneously. However, can anyone ever truly recall what they were thinking before that new thought?

I had been dealing with quite a bit of stress in my life lately. Finals, my job, and of course money; causing me to forget—a lot.

I was walking into my kitchen when I had one of those moments. *Why was I in here?* I stood there scratching my head as if it would make the thought appear. I began biting my cheek, squinting my eyes, when another thought flashed into my mind.

Kill it.

I stood there confused. Kill what? I shook my head and walked to the living room to watch some TV. I slumped down on the couch and began scrolling the channels—nothing looked interesting. When suddenly I remembered the frosted donuts, I had been walking to the kitchen for.

I got back up thinking about how delicious they were going to taste when I found myself at the silverware drawer—pulling out a steak knife. I laughed at myself. *I don't need a knife for the donuts.* I placed it back in the drawer and grabbed the box of frosted covered treats. As I made my way back to the couch my roommate's bird began chirping wildly.

I hated that bird. It would go off on a chirping tirade at all hours of the night; disrupting what little sleep I was getting these days. I rolled my eyes and turned up the volume on the TV. I must have dozed off. The next thing I remember was my roommate shaking me and asking where Ferdie was.

"What are you talking about man?" He's in his cage being his annoying ass self," I sarcastically replied.

"No dude, he's gone. Did you let him out? Why would you do that?"

I rubbed my eyes, "I didn't let him out, he was chirping away before I dozed off."

My roommate looked at me confused. "What do you mean dozed off? When I got home you were zoned out watching TV. I had to shake you back to reality."

I shook my head. "I was? Huh. I really don't remember anything before you started shaking me."

My roommate sighed and walked back to his room calling for Ferdie. I looked down at my hands and noticed the yellow feathers. Panic set in.

I raced to the bathroom to calm myself down as I gazed into the mirror. *You're losing your mind man.* I splashed some water onto my face and walked out.

I made my way to the kitchen where I saw the steak knife covered in blood and feathers. My heart started racing, rising up into my throat as I ran to the sink, puking up all the contents of my stomach. That's when I heard it, the voice in my head laughing at me. It came out as a thought, a thought that most people forget about.

This is where the demon resides. Stealing your innocence by turning your darkest thoughts, into realities. The second you find yourself too stressed out, where your mind races in all directions—that's when it strikes.

I butchered my roommates annoying bird with no recollection of doing so. The same thing could happen to anyone. The next time you enter a room forgetting why, walk right back out and keep forgetting. Calm your mind and ease your thoughts before the demon inside of you too, make sure you never forget again.

My House Is Haunted

Today, I woke up on an early Sunday morning in the springtime. It was just like any other day. The birds outside my window sang their sweet songs as the sun began to ascend, casting beautiful shadows as it went. I could smell the cherry blossoms as the breeze softly blew in through my open window.

Downstairs, I could hear my mother humming sweetly in the kitchen as she prepared breakfast, the smell of bacon drifting in through my door. I reached up and rubbed the sleep from my eyes, before hopping out of bed, pulling on an oversized sweatshirt, and walking out the door.

I bounded down the stairs, excited to fill my belly with whatever delicious meal my mother had prepared. As I rounded the corner to the kitchen, I found it empty, no sign of my mother or the delicious bacon I had smelled.

Confused, I called out to her. No reply.

I trotted back up the stairs and slowly creaked my parent's door open, it was empty. Panic began to rise in my gut. *Where were they?* I slumped out of the room and decided to check the garden. After I had pulled on my shoes I reached for the door, only to find it locked.

I tugged on it hard to no avail, it wouldn't budge. Feeling defeated I decided I would just call them. I picked up our home phone and began punching in their number. As I placed the phone to my ear, I realized there was no dial tone. I checked the cord to see if it had come unplugged, it hadn't.

As I placed the phone back down, I heard my mother singing again. Excited, I ran to the kitchen. Standing next to the stove cooking breakfast was a woman, a woman who was not my mother.

"Hey! Who are you and why are you here?" I shouted.

The woman continued flipping pancakes, completely ignoring me. Frustrated, I walked over to the stove, picking up a glass sitting on the counter next to her. As I raised it up, the woman let out a shrill scream and ran out of the kitchen. Leaving me standing there, glass still in hand with my mouth hanging open. *What the hell is going on,* I thought to myself.

I set the glass down and crept out of the kitchen in the direction the woman had run. As I reached the living room, I saw her sitting on the couch sobbing as a man I didn't know was consoling her. I slowly approached them when the man stiffened and shouted at me to leave them alone.

Terrified, I ran up the stairs into my bedroom and shut the door. I stayed there all day into the early evening, too terrified to leave. Around 6pm, there was a knock at the front door. I quietly opened my bedroom and looked down towards the front of the house.

A woman in black was standing just outside the door. The man and woman invited her in and she immediately looked right at me. I froze in shock as goosebumps began to rise all over my trembling body. *Who are these people?*

The man and woman guided their guest over to the kitchen table, where she began speaking to them in low, hushed tones. I tried my best to hear what she was saying, but it all sounded to foggy; as if she was speaking through a tunnel.

I decided to tiptoe down the stairs to get within a better hearing range. As I made my way to the wall separating myself from their view, I heard the woman call my name and asked me to join them. I shakily rounded the corner and froze.

They were all sitting in a circle holding hands as the woman in black had her eyes shut tight. I felt dizzy. *What was happening? Where were my parents?*

The woman spoke again, "Emily? Is that you?" I tried to say something, but my voice was too shaky to speak.

"Emily, why are you here? Please, speak to us so I can help you move on."

Move on? Move on from where? This is my house! I nervously walked over to the woman. "Wh—who are you guys? Why are you in my house?"

The woman stiffened. "She says this is her home," she spoke out loud to the parent imposters as if they couldn't hear me. I could feel the anger rising up into my gut. "This *is* my home!" I began to shout!

"Emily, Emily dear I'm going to need you to calm down. This is no longer your home and you need to leave Mr. and Mrs. Swanson alone. Do you hear me,

Emily? You need to leave." The woman pointed to the door as she spoke.

My world began to spin as my vision blurred, and then I remembered. I remembered that horrible Saturday night in the spring. It was dark out and my father had come home drunk; I could smell the intoxication on his breath. I remember being terrified as he hit my mother for a reason I didn't understand.

I had crawled under the table as he held her down, his hands around her neck. I remember her looking over at me with fear in her eyes, as she tried to motion for me to hide. With tears in mine, I ran for my bedroom.

Moments later my father busted in with a shotgun. "You little bitch," he slurred out. "Where are you, you little bitch!"

I was in my closet when he shot me. I remember hearing the loud crack of his gun as I felt the sharp pain ripping through my abdomen. As I laid there, fading in and out of consciousness, I heard one last bang—before closing my eyes forever, one last tear falling from my cheek.

Today, I woke up on an early Sunday morning in the springtime.

Cannibal Confessions

$\mathcal{W}$ELL, HELLO THERE. MY NAME IS BLAKE and it's very nice to meet you. I don't have much time left and I need to make a confession. So please bear with me.

I have killed approximately twenty-two people, including my own brother, if you even count him as human—he was very sick in the head. Anyways, my reason? They taste good. I know, I know, *ew*. Hear me out though. Have any of you actually *tried* human flesh before? My guess is no, and to that I say, don't knock it till you try it.

The best way to prepare a human is to first bathe the meat. I personally like to do a soak first with vinegar, it disinfects the body while also giving it a sweet tang once prepared. From there, you simply separate the joints, all of them; just pull and pull until you hear a satisfying *pop*—much like bubble wrap, really. It's quite fun.

Now that the body is clean and prepped, next in line is your cuts of meat. I prefer to start with the hands and the feet; get those out of the way and dispose of them properly. You can do this by using Soilex; generally, two boxes will do.

Bring a pot to boil and pour the boxes in, then carefully placed the appendages in the pot and wait about two hours. The Soilex should remove all the flesh, turning it into a jelly like-like substance that just rinses right off.

After that, it's basically just trial and error. Pick which part of the body you think would be the most appetizing; tenderize it, season it, and *poof*—you got yourself a fine meal. It pairs well with a delicate red blend and some oven roasted veggies.

Oh, and one more thing, make sure you dispose of the scraps the same way you disposed of the hands and feet. I would hate for you to be in the same position I am now. This recipe has been in my family for many generations and I fear I am the last. So now, I pass it on to you.

Bon appetit.

The Stalker

TWO DAYS AFTER I POSTED MY FIRST blog, I received a message. It was nothing out of the ordinary, just your usual, "Hey, I really like your story, can I use it for my podcast?" Feeling excited, as this was my first encounter with someone who seemed to enjoy my writing, I quickly responded, "Yes, of course!"

Two weeks passed, and I forgot all about the exchange. I decided I would wait to post another story for a few months and just enjoy reading instead. The months went by as I scrolled through story after story, reading in awe as I went—every author I found was just so talented.

When I finally felt ready to compose another story, I received a message alert within five minutes of hitting post. Again, it was someone asking to use it for their podcast. As I looked up at the username, I noticed it was the same person as before. Feeling a little more cautious, I decided to ask for their link before I agreed this time.

I had spaced out thinking about dinner, when my message alert pinged again. The user had replied with, "That is none of your concern, I just need your answer."

A bit taken aback, I replied with a simple, "No thank you," and left it at that.

Moments after I hit send, the user replied with, "Wrong answer."

I began to get really creeped out.

Who the hell is this freak?

I decided to block him and shake off the stalker vibe that itched in the back of my mind.

One month after the strange encounter, I began writing my next story.

Wow, this is a lot harder to do one handed, I thought to myself, as phantom pains shot through the now vacant space at the end of my arm. I had a slight … cooking accident about a month ago that had left me mildly "inconvenienced", you could say.

Once I finished, I was having a tough time deciding on the perfect title. I began jotting down all of the headlines deemed suitable on a separate doc. As I was checking them over, eliminating the inadequate ones, I received a notification from my blog saying I had a new message.

As I opened it up, my blood ran cold as a shiver made its way down my spine.

"I like the third title best. Use it."

I sat there in shock for a while, mouth hanging open.

H—how the fuck?

I immediately clicked back to my doc with the titles, making sure it was set to private.

It was.

I went back to my blog and made sure to block the user, again. Feeling massively violated, I shut off my computer and decided to watch some TV. A couple hours had passed, when I received a knock at my door. I quickly jumped up to see who was there and found a cheeky UPS man on the other side—holding a package.

Confused, as I hadn't ordered anything recently, I reached for the knob—slowly opening it. The delivery man shoved a clipboard at me to sign, handed me the package, and went on his merry way.

First thing I noticed was that the return address was the same as my own.

This guy is really getting ballsy.

I grabbed the box cutters out of the drawer in the kitchen and shakily began to open the strange parcel.

As soon as I had it partially opened, a metallic stench began to fill my nostrils. I immediately closed the lid and pushed it to the side, I knew what the package concealed. Feeling more anger than I have felt in a long time, I walked straight over to my computer, unblocked the creep, and began composing a message.

If you do not stop harassing me, I am going to cut off your other hand, and send that one to your mom.

There has been no reply since.

We Will Return

LAST YEAR, MY PARENTS WENT THROUGH a nasty divorce. I eventually made the decision to stay with my mom, but my dad had requested the house, which meant we had to move.

We quickly stumbled upon a beautiful house in Boston. It was huge! Way more space than we needed but it was the right price and the sale went quickly. Almost too quickly.

My mother was an ER nurse and worked nights, which left me alone often. I really didn't mind, I like my privacy, but when strange things started to happen, I quickly changed my mind. It was little things at first. The TV would turn on by itself, doors would burst open without anyone there, the floors would creak at night as if someone was walking on them. Typical old house spooks that end up being nothing more than an overactive imagination.

Until one night while my mother was at work, I was laying in my bed reading a Tolstoy novel when I thought I heard footsteps just outside my door. I quickly sat up and looked at the crack underneath the door waiting to see my mom's shoes, they weren't there. Instead, I saw the bathroom light turn on.

I waited silently. A few minutes later, the bathroom light turned back off, but there were no footsteps. I called out to my mother with no reply. I got up and walked over to my door, opening it and calling out to her again.

Silence.

I crept down the stairs to look for her car, but our driveway was empty. I walked around to all the doors to make sure they were locked; they were. Convinced I was seeing things, I started to make my way back up to my room when a shadow in the kitchen caught my eyes.

When I looked towards it a figure came stomping down the hallway towards me. I let out a shriek, as I threw my hands up to my face to shield myself. My heart pounding in my chest as I waited for the impact.

Nothing.

I slowly opened my eyes, to find myself alone. I released the breath I had been holding and booked it up the stairs into my room. I shut the door behind me, locked it, and called my mom.

As I told her everything that had happened, I frantically begged her to come home. She sighed and told me to just turn off the scary movies and go to bed. Before I could protest, my mother said she loved me, and the line went dead.

Feeling defeated, I slumped down on my bed rubbing my temples, trying to decide what the hell had just happened. Then I heard a piano begin to play. It was an eerie sound that made the hair on the back of my neck raise. I went to get up when I remembered something crucial—we don't own a piano.

I laid my head on my pillow, pulled the covers up to my chin and closed my eyes. I never found sleep that night as I laid awake listening to song after song coming from a nonexistent instrument.

As soon as the sun peeked through my bedroom window, the music stopped. I got up to find that my mom had not yet returned home. I grabbed my phone as it lit up with a voicemail, she had left me. I quickly played it. Sadness swept over me as I heard her say she would be pulling a double and wouldn't be home until that evening. How did I miss that call?

I huffed down to the kitchen to pour myself a bowl of cereal, I was famished. As I rounded the corner, I saw that all the kitchen cabinets were open. *What the hell is going on?* No longer hungry I decided I would take a shower.

I made my way to the bathroom hoping the hot water would help wash off the weirdness of the night before. As I went to step in, I noticed a dark spot on the back of my leg. I reached down to wipe whatever it was off, when pain shot through me.

As I turned my leg to the side to get a better view, I froze. It was a bruise of a handprint. I felt cold and violated. Was there really someone in my house? I turned off the shower, wrapped a towel around me and slowly crept out of the bathroom.

I grabbed my old softball bat and starting yelling to whoever was there to show themselves. As I rounded the corner to the stairs a picture frame fell off the wall and shattered. I let out another loud shriek, ran to the coat closet, and locked myself inside. I was going to wait there until my mom got home.

I ended up falling asleep. I began to dream about the door to my mother's room. In my dream I reached out to open it, but it was locked. A thought crossed my mind; was it keeping something in, or was it keeping something out. I immediately woke up to the closet door handle wiggling. I thought I was going to hyperventilate, but when it burst open there stood my mother.

I began shouting at her and telling her there was someone in our house and that we needed to leave. At first, she looked at me as though I was crazy until I showed her the bruise on my leg. She began searching the house and found nothing. No signs that anyone had ever been there besides us.

She sat me down on the couch and sighed. She told me that she didn't want to spook me when we bought our house, so she kept a few minor details about the sale from me.

Apparently, the house was a foreclosure. The previous owners had been slaughtered in their bedrooms while they slept. Scary part was, the couple had a young daughter whom the police were never able to locate.

In the room where they were murdered, written on the wall in their blood were the words, "we will return," over and over again.

When the case ran cold, the house was boarded up and kept off the market. Until last year. My mom walked over to a chest and pulled out the newspaper clipping of the incident. It was all real.

I looked at my mother with betrayal in my eyes and told her I wanted to live with Dad. She obliged and I never went back to that house again, although I did have reoccurring dreams of doing so.

After I left, things became increasingly worse. It was as if whatever occupied that house was angry at my departure. My mother quickly put the house on the market and moved into an apartment close to our old home.

Looking back, I do kind of feel bad for leaving her like that, but I wasn't about to wait around and see who was going to return.

The Dream Whisperer

$\mathcal{I}$ GREW UP IN AN EXTREMELY SMALL TOWN in Oregon called Astoria. Most of you only know its location on a map simply because of *The Goonies*, and while that movie is phenomenal, it is not the only thing my town is known for.

In the last month, I decided I was going to do my senior thesis on our town's history. Since then I've spent most of my time in our local library, digging up everything I could about Astoria's past. Yesterday, I eventually found my way to the artifacts section, located all the way in the back of the ancient building, covered in an inch of dust.

After sifting through hundreds of binders filled with old newspaper clippings, something caught my eye. At the very bottom of one of the shelves, there was a red binder, completely hidden behind the support beam. I had to really dig to get it out, and once I did, a thick cloud of dust temporarily muddled my vision.

Upon settling, I was able to examine the binder more closely. It looked to be about a hundred years old, but practically in perfect condition, as if it had not been held in quite a few decades. As I opened it up, I realized only one article was kept inside, a newspaper clipping from the early 1900s.

Immediately feeling as though it was hidden for a reason, I peeked over my shoulder, finding the only nearby sound, was that of my heart thudding rapidly in my chest. I glanced back down at the newspaper article and began reading:

> *May 7, 1919*
>
> *After a week of mysterious disappearances and murders, Astoria's notorious killer known as The Dream Whisperer, is still at large. One young girl lives, to tell the story.*

As I pulled open my phone to check the time, I shuddered when my eyes found the date instead, April 29, 2019. Exactly one hundred years from today. I placed my phone back in my pocket and continued reading:

> *"Sally Mae recalls falling asleep in her bed at 9:30 p.m. and waking up five hours later in the middle of the woods. While she has no recollection of how she managed to walk eight miles from her home, she says she remembers the whispers.*
>
> *In her dreams, she saw a man she referred to as* 'Psíthyros Thánato'. *She states he was a shadow man with no face who knew her by name, yet never physically spoke to her. Instead, he calmly whispered to her in her mind as he showed her the tragic death she would soon endure.*
>
> *Nearby campers found her in a catatonic state, repeating the words, 'I must die.'*
>
> *Given this new lead, it is clear that the suspect uses an opiate on his victims, leaving them in a hallucinogenic state in which he can better manipulate his murders. Everyone is advised to stay indoors after sundown, and triple lock their homes.*
>
> *Who knows when he will strike again."*

I quickly closed the book, and bounded towards the middle of the library, I had to get on a computer to look all of this up. As I googled steadily for over an hour, I came up empty. There was simply no mention of the murders or even about Sally Mae, it was as if she never existed.

Already having tucked the binder into my bag, I made my way to the door, and headed towards our history museum. If anyone would know about these strange murders, it would be our town historian; James Haltly. I crossed the street, quickly making my way to the front entrance doors, where I saw James enthusiastically talking to some tourists about *The Goonies.*

Having heard his spiel hundreds of times, I rolled my eyes as I hastily walked towards him, cutting him off mid-sentence. The couple gave me rude glances, that I thoroughly enjoyed ignoring, as I pulled James to the side.

"What can you tell me about the Dream Whisperer," I blurted out.

I noticed the sudden shift in Mr. Haltly's demeanor. His earlier enthusiasm quickly faded from his face, replaced by an expression one can only describe as true terror.

"Where did you hear that name, son? And who else have you told?"

I looked Mr. Haltly over for minute, studying his face for any sign that he was pulling my leg.

He wasn't.

"I … I found this in the library," I finally replied, pulling out the dusty red binder from my backpack. Mr. Haltly's face turned stark white as I placed it in his hands.

"No, no, no!" he recited over and over while shaking his head. "I knew I should have burned this damn thing years ago! Stupid, stupid, stupid!"

I stood there watching the historian beat himself up for a good ten minutes before a glimpse of hope spread across his face.

"Who else did you tell?" he blurted out, grabbing my shoulders with urgency.

"No one, sir. I just found it," I managed to choke out, before he quickly escorted me to his back office.

"Take a seat, son," James said sternly as he walked to the other side of his desk. As soon as I was seated, he reached into a drawer and pulled out a bottle of scotch—pouring himself a good-sized glass before returning the bottle back to its hidden resting place. I waited patiently for him to tell me what the hell was going on, but it was clear that he was struggling to find the words as he sipped long and hard on his liquid courage.

"You have to forget," Mr. Haltly suddenly blurted out. "You have to forget his name, and everything you read, you have to. Do you hear me? No one else must know his name!"

He slammed his fist on the desk as he stared daggers into my soul. I swallowed audibly, causing Haltly to lean back in his chair as he smoothed over what little hair he had left.

"Wh—what is he?" I finally managed to mumble.

The historian looked at me as if he was having a battle within himself and I, being the cause of such abuse. When he pulled the scotch back out, I shifted in my seat, preparing to not waste anymore of my time, but he gestured for me to stay put. Then, he spoke.

"I can't tell you for sure who or what he is, I do however, know he feeds on nightmares. He fed on my baby brother and he was never seen alive again. That was almost fifty years ago."

I sat there in shock at what I was hearing. "Did you say fifty years ago? Is there a record of his disappearance?"

"No! Dammit," Haltly yelled. "I told you I got rid of everything! Well, almost everything." He sighed as he gestured towards the book. "He lives underground, beneath the city," I heard him mumble. "My guess is he has been there since before the city was ever built. All I know is, every fifty years or so he gets to … well, he gets to feed."

He looked at me with guilt in his eyes. I pondered this for a moment, trying to put the pieces in my head. I glanced at the calendar on his desk and my blood ran cold.

"You say he comes out every fifty years? This article states that the disappearances started happening a week from May 7th. That means … that means," I tried to get the words out.

"Yes, that means he will awake some time tonight." Mr. Haltly sighed and looked out the window of his office.

I gathered my things and told James that I needed to go. Before I left his office, he looked completely defeated and again begged me not to tell a soul. I assured him I wouldn't.

I went straight home. If I was only one of two people who knew about the Dream Whisperer, I was in danger, and wanted to spend as much time with my family as I could.

I played board games with my siblings, helped mom bake a pie, and I even let dad talk about football with me for over an hour. I hid the tears throughout the day until it was bedtime. Making sure to kiss all of them goodnight first, before heading to my room, counting my last steps as I went. I crept into bed and waited. Waited for sleep to come and take my mind away with the night.

But sleep never came.

An hour had passed before I heard a crunch come from my closet, sending shivers down my spine. I slowly stood from my bed, breath coming out in quick jolts as I made my way to my closet door. I reached for the handle, willing my body to move and face the demon.

The door flew open before I had the chance to muster up the confidence. I jumped back in surprise, only to find my little sister giggling up at me. I sighed. "What are you doing in my room, Lucy? You need to go back to bed."

She stuck her tongue out at me, "Fine! Your closet stinks anyways. Here, take your stupid book back, it's lame."

I stared down at the red book Lucy handed me before she sulked off to her room. Fear began to pour from my veins as the reality of what just happened raced through my mind. She knew. My little sister knew his name. I began to feel lightheaded as my whole world began to shatter around me.

"No, not Lucy, please. No," was all I got out before the room faded to black.

***

I awoke this morning with a newfound appreciation for the life that was almost taken from me. You see, the Dream Whisperer came to me last night and told me about his plans for the future. He's tired of my boring little town and would like to, "spread his wings," if you will. He promised to pardon my sister of her eternal nightmare if I told others his name.

He looks forward to meeting all of you very soon.

The Fairy Garden

My sister Mia and I grew up in an old farmhouse out in the backwoods of Texas. It was a rundown place—forgotten, but home, nonetheless.

It was just us and our father. Our mother had walked out on us just two days after I turned nine, Mia was seven. We never heard from her again. Our father seemed so lost without her for days. We heard him in his room at night still talking to her as if she was there.

A few months later, my dad's friend Maggie came to stay with us. He said he needed help while he was at work, and we needed to listen to her while he was gone. We didn't much care for Maggie though.

She was always glaring at us and lying to our father, telling him we pulled her hair, or hit her—anything to get us in trouble. Per usual, our father would always believe her and send us outside to play, telling us he would think up a punishment later.

We spent most of our summers outside anyways; playing in the warm sunshine, while enjoying the cool breeze that smelled of cherry blossoms. We were always searching for new places to explore, new trees to climb, but you could almost always find us in our Fairy Garden.

While on one of our many adventures, probably pretending to be explorers in search of some exotic animal, we stumbled across a flower patch. It was the most beautiful thing we had ever seen.

There had to be about a dozen different kinds of flowers that grew from this little patch, with a row of mushrooms sprouting in the middle. We began collecting little pebbles to place along the outside, thus creating our little fairy garden.

We would spend hours each day there, making up stories about princess fairies and all the grand balls they would throw in their mushroom palace.

Our favorite fairy was named Sophia, she had long, golden sunshine hair, just like our mama. We would pretend that she would take us to her castle

THE FAIRY GARDEN

and let us stay with her forever. She loved us so much.

One summer morning we awoke to pouring down rain, which meant we had to stay inside with Maggie. She was the absolute worst. That particular day we had to clean the toilets with toothbrushes. The whole time she stood over us, drinking wine with her smug evil face. I hated her.

Later that night, Mia suggested we sneak out to our Garden and make sure it didn't flood. We got dressed in our warmest clothes and tip toed out the back door. As we approached the garden, we saw that the water had made the flowers grow unbelievably tall.

We weaved our way to the middle of the patch where the mushroom palace was, only to have our hopes crushed. The mushrooms had disappeared and in their place was a little black swamp. It smelled awful. We plugged our noses as we bent down to inspect it further.

My eyes began to water, and my hand wasn't doing a very good job of masking the smell—we slowly backed away. Mia started to cry as I pulled her into me and walked back to the house. I told her we would find another fairy garden to explore in the morning.

When I awoke the next day, Mia wasn't in her bed. I ran downstairs and asked Maggie if she had seen her, only to get a shrug and an eye roll—typical. I ran outside and called for her. A couple minutes later, I heard giggling coming from the back yard, followed by Mia calling my name.

I knew where she was.

I sprinted over to our fairy garden and screamed. Mia was inside of the smelly bog, playing with one of her dolls. Startled, she looked up at me and asked what was wrong.

I began to shake, as tears streamed down my face. Sticking out of the ground beside the goo, was a patch of golden sunshine hair. My little sister wasn't playing in a bog, she was playing in—*our mother.*

Unknown Number

$\mathcal{W}$HAT YOU ARE ABOUT TO READ WAS recovered from a burnt phone I found while on a hike. I was unable to track down its owner, but felt his story needed to be heard.

***

Almost a month ago to this day, the government sent out a mass warning to Hawaii residents about a nuclear threat. Don't believe me, look it up. While the warning was deemed false, the repercussions were not.

You see, two weeks ago I received a text message from a number I did not recognize asking me if I had made it out safely. I hastily responded with the typical, "New number, who dis?" Five minutes later I received a response that sent chills down my spine. This is a transcription of our messages.

Unknown: *Hey man, I don't know what is happening right now, tell me you survived! Almost everyone is dead!*

Me: *Who is this? What are you talking about? Survived what?*

Unknown: *What do you mean who is this? It's Matt, how did you survive the bomb??*

Me: *What bomb? Who the hell is this?*

Now, while my best friend's name is in fact Matt, I had personally just gone out with Matt for beers last week. So, figuring it had to be someone fucking with me, I decided to humor them.

Me: *Okay, "Matt", what bomb are you talking about and where the fuck are you?*

Matt: *What do you mean what bomb? Dude where are you, and how did you survive? I'm freaking out! My dad's friend called him on his solar-powered phone and told him there were people outside eating other people. Do not go outside man, it's terrifying.*

Okay, by this point I knew it was a prank. Eating other people? Come on.

Me: *Ha Ha, who is this, this isn't The Walking Dead man ....*

Unknown: *What the fuck are you talking about!! This isn't some joke fuckface, look outside.*

At this point I was thoroughly confused, so as you would guess, I looked outside. Before me was my neighbor, Thomas, teaching his daughter how to ride a bike. I must have watched them for five or ten minutes. She pedaled while Thomas held onto the seat cheering her on as if he wasn't helping her along.

I gave up and walked back to my couch. I sat there and thought a moment before I decided to just text my friend Matt. Maybe he would know who the hell was playing this elaborate prank and why.

Me: *Man, who did you give my number to, and why are they texting me about Walker's?*

Matt: *Haha, what are you talking about, I'm working right now, I didn't give anyone your number.*

Confused, I decided to text the imposter and figure this shit out.

Me: *Okay bro, I'm done with this shit. Do not text me again!*

Unknown: *What the fuck man, I'm not fucking around! If you haven't, lock your house down and stay where you are, I'll come get you!*

I'll admit I was a little spooked, but I decided to wait, to wait to see if the prankster would show up at my door so I could kick their ass for wasting my time with this stupid charade.

Thirty minutes passed.

Me: *So uhhh where are you, bro? Did you get lost?*

No reply

Me: *Mmk, whoever the fuck this is, don't text me again, this is lame.*

I decided to look closer at the number to try and figure out who it might be. I quickly became confused. Where there should have been numbers, there were symbols:

⊤ ⊢ — ≡ ∴ ∇.

Puzzled, I decided to google it. Nothing came up. It had to be some kind of weird hacker, right?

Me: *Okay, who the fuck is this and how did you get my number?*

Unknown: *Ghrlp Mr*

Two minutes after that text, there was a knock at my door. Nervously, I peeked out the little window at the top. Before me were two men, dressed all in black, standing on my porch.

"Are you Frank Hatcher? We need you to step outside," they sternly demanded from the other side. I slowly pulled the door open, looking at them awkwardly and confused. Again, they spoke.

"Frank, we are going to need you to step outside." As I inched forward, they immediately asked for my cell phone. Anxiously, I handed it to them and stared as they immediately took it from my grasp. As soon as they had it in their possession, they asked me if I had received any strange messages. Now, I've watched enough CSI to know that the correct answer was no. Upon telling them as such, they gave me a suspicious look and nodded to each other. While still holding onto my cell phone, they returned back to their cars.

I stood on my porch dumbfounded at the fact they took my phone with zero explanation. before I could work up the courage to march down to their vehicles, they quickly opened their doors and headed back up to me. As they handed my phone back, they hastily told me I needed to go with them. As it seems I didn't have much of a choice in the matter, I did. I opened up my phone and clicked on my message icon to get a closer look at the conversation between, "Matt" and I.

It was gone.

I couldn't see out the windows of the car that they had practically forced me into, so I honestly have no idea where they took me or even what direction we were going.

After what felt like hours, we finally arrived at some run-down warehouse. So, this is where I die, I kept thinking to myself. I should have never given them my damn phone. I should have slammed the door right in their smug, intimidating faces and booked it out of there.

The two men got out of the car and opened my door, motioning for me to step out and follow them. I thought about making a break for it. I ran track in High School, I could probably outrun them. However, I could not outrun the Glocks strapped to their hips, so I followed. As we walked into the warehouse, I noticed that it was empty. Completely vacant of all furniture and people.

The only thing that stood out was an elevator on the other side of the building. As soon as we approached it, one of the guys pulled out a badge and scanned it on the operator pad; where you choose up or down. I'm guessing he chose down.

The elevator lit up and with a soft, "ding" as it opened. We stepped inside and I immediately felt the tension. I began to sweat and realized I had been holding my breath. I knew this would probably be the end for me as soon as we reached wherever this devil box went to. I continued to hold my breath and wait for the descent. It never came. Instead, the other side of the elevator opened, and I was herded like a blind pig into a room full of black suits sitting behind computers.

There was a big screen in front of them that had a live picture of what looked to be a city but desolated. Confused, I turned towards the two men to ask them what the hell was going on when a tall lanky looking man approached us. He had a big bald head but a rather glorious beard that I was actually a little envious of. Baldy was dressed all in black and had a walk that demanded authority.

"You must be Frank Thatcher! My name is Mac Brown, it's an absolute pleasure to meet you," he declared, as he reached for my hand.

"Yeah ... I can't say the same. What the hell is this? Why am I here? Who are you guys?" I replied as I stuck my hand into my pocket, dismissing his handshake of lies.

Placing his hand back at his side as well, he studied the annoyed expression that was clearly planted on my face and gestured for me to take a seat. "Son, I'm going to give it to you straight. I know this all may be very confusing for you, but we need your help in locating Matthew. We are not yet sure how he was able to reach you, but we need to ask him some questions."

Flustered, I began to tell him how I had no idea who this Matt guy was. I stressed that it was someone pretending to be my real friend Matt to mess with me for God knows why. Mac sat in silence, listening to me vent my frustrations. He almost seemed to be studying my every move, as if I was lying or like he was waiting for me to slip up. I began to ask him if I could leave, when a black suit walked over and whispered into Mac's ear. They both turned towards the big screen. I followed their gaze and my mouth dropped open as I stared at the screen in disbelief.

Most of the buildings in the broadcasted view of the city were partially destroyed; rubble was everywhere. Right smack in the middle of all the chaos I distinctly made out a shape of a man, but he looked disheveled; something was off. As I looked closer, I noticed his mouth was moving, chomping almost, was he biting the air? I couldn't believe what I was seeing. I squinted harder and noticed the flesh on his face was all fucked up, causing me to recoil in horror as I realized what I was looking at. Zombies. I was looking at a fucking *zombie!*

Mac noticed my shocked state and spoke very carefully; I will never forget what he said. "Yes Frank, what you are witnessing is real. The missile that was headed for Hawaii contained a virus that caused this—this, undead situation and it seems as though Terra X is in distress. We are worried that the terrorist organization—ILF—could be working on a similar virus, here. Therefore it is so important that you help us find Matthew, as he is somehow not infected."

I stood there for a good five minutes, mouth hanging open like an idiot while my mind raced. When I finally found my voice, I yelled, "What the hell is going on? The missile threat was a mistake! An accident! What the fuck do you mean, "Terra X"? As in what, another Earth. You cannot be serious. Is this some kind of joke? Where are the cameras? I think this has gone on long enough."

I'll admit, I lost my cool. I was freaking out. None of what Mac said made any rational sense. Zombies aren't real, there is no such thing as Terra X, and "Matt" was probably just some lonely guy in his mom's basement getting a good chuckle out of scaring random strangers. Mac and the others let me have my meltdown.

As I collected myself, I asked them if I could just go home. I told them I wouldn't tell anyone about their weird ass fright factory, or about their strange conspiracy theories if they would just let me leave. They all stood there, looking at me with almost a hint of sadness in their eyes.

Mac, placing an unwanted hand on my shoulder, broke the silence. "We can't let you go home Frank, like I said before, we need you to help us find Matthew. He has the answers we need, and you are going to go get them, as he somehow has a connection to you."

I must have passed out because I woke up in a random room, with white walls and nothing but a couch and a table. On top of the table was a note, reminding me that while they had let me keep my phone, I mustn't tell anyone about the operation at hand.

These people were either bat shit crazy and I was going to be turned into some mental experiment, or they were telling the truth and I was really going to be dropped off on some Earth that's been taken over by the walking dead.

I picked up my phone and began texting my family. I caught up on their lives and in a subtle way, I let all of them know how much I loved them. It was the hardest thing I have ever had to do, and I fell asleep with tears in my eyes. The next morning, I made the impetuous walk back to the main room of the warehouse. As I rounded the last corner, I felt the warm, electric glow that seemed to be coming from the back of the room. There was a portal of some sort.

Mac approached me with a hazmat looking suit and told me to put it on over my clothes. As I did, I noticed no one else was suiting up. "What is this Mac? I thought you guys were coming with me," I half shouted. I caught a slight expression of worry from him, before he changed back to his authoritative self. "We uh—we need to stay behind and help you from here. We will have full eyes on you through the monitor, as well as your suit." You are lying coward, I thought to myself. As I approached the portal, I turned and told Mac that if anything happened to me, he better let my family know and compensate them somehow. He gave me a nod, and with that, I entered. The best way I can describe the journey is electrifying.

Upon entering, I felt a vibration rupture throughout my whole body. It started in my hands, spread to my lower half, then jolted into my head. It was too bright for me to keep my eyes open; think of a moment where headlights are coming towards you, head on, on a dark empty street—blinding you immediately. I felt as though I was falling, falling into an ibis of nothing at an impossible rate. What was only a moment felt like an eternity.

The falling sensation came to a sudden halt as I stumbled forward. I felt dizzy and immediately hunched over and hurled all of the contents in my stomach. As I regained my composure, I nervously opened my eyes to what lay before me. Just as I had witnessed on the monitor; the land was desolate. This word had a sepia feel to it—everything was hazy and enveloped in a dust cloud. I pulled out my phone and sent "Matt" a quick text. "Hey man, where are you?"

Nothing.

I began to panic as my heart thudded deep in my chest. Was all of this for nothing? Was Matt already dead? Why didn't we message him before I left?

Suddenly, my phone vibrated. A rush of relief spread throughout me. "Frank! You are still alive! When I hadn't heard from you, I thought the worst! Send me your location and I will come find you, sit tight man."

I proceeded to find some sort of cover under what I assumed to be an old bridge, and pinged Matt my location. A short while later I heard someone ruffling through the debris above me. Silently, I crept out from my hiding place and slowly peered over the side of the bridge. It was not Matt. It was a man dressed in a rundown suit that was torn up pretty bad. I looked down at his leg and noticed a bone was protruding out of the side, as brownish green goo leaked from it.

As I made my way to his face, I cringed. His flesh looked as if it was melting off and infected. I'm sure if I didn't have the suit on, I would have smelled the putrid essence of a decaying body. He whipped his head back and forth, letting out a deep growl that sounded like someone drowning as he chomped at the air ferociously. I immediately tucked myself back into my cubby beneath the bridge and held my breath.

UNKNOWN NUMBER

I could feel my heart in my throat as I closed my eyes and prayed, cursing Mac at the same time. I thought I heard the "man" walk towards the end of the bridge and then it was silent.

As I began to open my eyes, a hand grabbed at me and began pulling me up. I screamed and flailed my arms, grabbing at air, kicking whatever I could to regain my ground. Two hands grabbed my shoulders and shook me. It was Matt! He held a finger to his mouth silencing my screams and motioned for me to follow him quietly. I trailed just behind him as we made our way to an alleyway.

When we were finally out of sight, he sat down and pulled out some sort of hand drawn map.

"Dude, what is going on? Was that really a fucking zombie? What are you doing? We have to get out of here!" I began to plead. Matt looked up at me questionably.

"What do you mean what is going on? How do you not know? Where were you when the missile hit? Did your family survive? We need to get to the safety mark here on the map, it's the town hall. I believe that is where survivors will gather -,"

I cut him off. I began to tell him about who I really was and why I was here. As I told him everything I knew, he looked up at me in shock and disbelief, mouth gaping open. When I finished, he just sat there in silence. I spoke again.

"Matt. Man, I'm really sorry to say this, but it seems as if you are the only survivor. We have to get out of here." He sat there, trying to dissect everything I had just told him. I swear, he went through all the emotions of loss within five minutes until he finally reached acceptance.

He stood and replied, "Ok, now what?"

I told him that he could come back to my Earth with me and we would figure it all out together. He seemed to accept that answer and began packing away his map. As soon as he zipped his bag, we heard the growls. I peeked around the corner and saw five of the undead coming right for us. Matt reached up and grabbed a ladder that was hanging from a stairwell and we ascended to the top. We climbed until we reached the roof of the building and crouched down with our backs to the wall.

"Can those bastards climb?" I shrieked out.

"No man, we should be safe up here for now. I say we wait it out awhile until after dark. I have some black out goggles with night vision I scooped up from a rundown tech store in the city a few days ago."

I nodded and leaned back against the wall, hitting my head a little harder than I intended. As I reached up to rub it, I remembered I was wearing a suit. If said suit was mandatory it must mean that the virus was still in the air. I looked over at Matt and wondering how he was still—human. He was sitting back eating a Snickers and humming with his eyes closed. He looked identical to my Matt back on earth, but maybe a little more grounded. I guess an apocalypse will do that to you.

I decided I better check in with Mac. While he couldn't talk to me, we had a button system; green for when I was ready to come back home so he could open up the portal. Red, in case I had been infected, and yellow to tell him I was cautiously making my way back. I pressed yellow. I must have dozed off because I was awakened by Matt kicking me in the foot, telling me it was time to head out.

He handed me a pair of goggles and helped me turn on the night vision before we climbed back down the stairs and made our way to the end of the alley. He pointed to the bridge I had previously been hiding under and counted on his fingers, one two three. We sprinted across the opening and dashed back into my hiding place. I pushed the green button and a loud bang erupted in front of us as the portal opened. We both ran through and were immediately back at my Earth.

Matt, not aware of the effects of the portal, heaved up his Snickers bar upon entrance. When I looked around, I realized we were in some sort of tent. Mac must have sheltered the portal while I was gone as a safety precaution. I began to take off my suit when Mac's voice came through on an intercom.

"Welcome back Frank, you have done exceptionally! Matt, welcome to Earth. I know it has been a long journey for both of you, my team is assembled to run some tests before you both can get a good dinner in you and debrief." Matt looked over at me and shrugged. We made our way through the tent to a door.

There was a sign taped to the wall that asked us to strip down before entering the room on the other side. As we entered, we were immediately showered in burning hot water and then sprayed with what I assumed to be some sort of decontamination mist. The door in front of us opened and clothes were laid out on a chair for us to put on.

A team of black suits dressed in hazmat approached us and began running all sorts of tests. I'm surprised I had as much blood to give as they took. When they were done, we were allowed to exit the tent, where we were greeted by a room of applause. Everyone cheered and hollered, and we were slapped on the back as we made our way to Mac.

He quickly began to go further into detail about why we needed Matt here on this earth and about the virus. Matt quietly listened and occasionally nodded. Dinner was brought out for us and we filled our empty stomachs while Mac continued to talk.

He filled Matt in about the ILF and how they may be planning a biological attack. Matt looked at him incredulously and told him that the ILF weren't the ones who caused the epidemic, some facility in the eastern hemisphere was. Mac cut him off abruptly and told us that we both looked exhausted.

Shortly after, we were both sent to bed. I'm not sure how Matt slept, but I slept like a baby. The next morning, Mac ushered in some breakfast for us. On my tray was a vaccine.

"Frank, since you were the one brave enough to rescue Matt—potentially saving everyone on our Earth, I want you to have the first super vaccine we have concocted from Matt's DNA. It will protect you against a possible biological attack," Mac said with enthusiasm.

I looked down at the vaccine in front of me.

"You mean you want me to be a test dummy, right?" I mocked.

Matt chuckled. "You really are just like the Frank on Terra X."

I rolled my eyes and nodded towards Mac.

After he inoculated me, four other men entered and began checking my vitals. I fucking knew it. After they were done, they nodded towards Mac and he excitedly clapped his hands together and practically skipped out of our room.

I looked over at Matt who was eating his bacon and eggs enthusiastically and asked him how he was feeling. I mean, he must be pretty broken up over everything that happened, right? Apparently not. On his Earth, his parents had died, and I was really the only person in his immediate life. I felt sad for him. As I reached over to express my condolences, I got a good look at his eyes.

"Wait, hold still a second." I whispered nervously. I looked closer. The whites of his eyes had gold flecks in them, nothing like I had ever seen before. I immediately ran into the bathroom and looked in the mirror. I too, now had gold flecks in the whites of my eyes. I stumbled back into our room, heart racing. What did this mean? Why had my eyes changed? And then I heard the growls. The same growls I had heard on Terra X and I knew we had made a mistake.

While Matt may have been the only person to survive because of some immunity to the virus—an immunity I too carried somehow. It apparently did not mean he wasn't a carrier. I looked over at Matt who was still enjoying his breakfast, when the door flew open. A flood of the undead swept in—all wearing black suits. Matt dropped his plate, then looked at me with panic in his eye.

What the fuck have I done?

It seemed as though Mac and his crew of black suits, injected themselves with the vaccine concocted from Matt's DNA. When I didn't show any obvious side-effects, they thought they would be in the clear—they were obviously wrong.

Fuck, fuck, fuck.

I immediately ran over to his dropped plate of food, arming myself with the butter knife he had used to cut his bacon. I know, not the best weapon but, what are you gonna do? Matt however, having done this before, broke a leg off of the table in the back of the room—nodding in my direction. He was prepared for this fight.

The black suits began charging all at once, backing us into a corner. Matt aggressively grabbed my arm, ushering me into the bathroom. He propped the table leg in a way that would jam the door shut, while yelling for me to find a way out as he held it in place.

"There! The air vents!" I pointed. Matt looked up.

"Perfect, give me a boost!" As he let go of the door, I grabbed his foot and unsteadily helped him up towards the ceiling. He began to push on the vent to make it cave—he was successful. As soon as he was in, he reached down and grabbed my hand, but missed—just as the zombies broke through the door.

Frantically, I leaped for his arms again to no avail. I started to panic. Matt yelled at me to try one more time, but fear was leaving me paralyzed. I quickly snapped out of it right before one of them tried to make a meal out of my arm. Matt reached and grabbed my hand, pulling me up to safety.

We crawled around several corners before we finally found a room that appeared empty; the kitchen I presumed. We opened the vent and climbed down, checking every angle for the zombie fuckers as we dropped. It was all clear.

We silently ran to the back of the room, checking our backs the whole way, until we found the door. As we walked through it I was caught off guard, smacking directly into a force of rotting flesh. I let out a—less than manly shriek, as I fell backwards with the zombie toppling down on me—biting at my face. Matt grabbed a butcher knife off the counter and punched it into the black suit's head, causing horrendous smelling sludge to ooze onto my face. I held my breath and pushed the walker off of me as I staggered to my feet.

"Wh—why would you do that? What if we can change them back? You just possibly killed a man!" I shouted.

"Are you serious? I just saved your fucking life! We don't have time for this, come on!" Matt retorted back.

I quickly followed him down the hall, and into the back of the warehouse, still questioning his actions. We were approaching the doors, when a thought occurred to me—what happens if they get out? I grabbed Matt's arm before he opened the door that would lead us to safety.

"Wait man, we can't just leave. We have to do something about this before it spreads. I don't want my Earth to end up like Terra X." As Matt sneered at me, I knew he disagreed.

"What is that supposed to mean? None of this is our fault, not our problem to fix!" He shouted back. "I wasn't going to tell you this but, on Terra X, it was Mac's team who launched the Missile. They covered it up by blaming it on terrorists. I thought just maybe—maybe they were the opposite of the jerks on my Earth. I was wrong"

I stared at him—trying to find a flaw in his story but, it all made sense. "So, they just wanted your

DNA to make themselves immune? They weren't going to give it to everyone?"

Matt looked down, "No man, they weren't. I knew it as soon as he cut me off yesterday."

"Well, we still have to do something. We can't let them win. We have to fix this!" I began to plead.

With anger in his eyes, Matt yanked his arm away and ran out the door—leaving me all alone.

"Coward!" I yelled after him, but he wasn't wrong, none of this was our fault. I stood there for a few moments trying to figure out how to make this all go away. I could try to round them all up into one room, and call someone, but who? Then it hit me—the gas stove! I could blow this place up; exterminate all the zombies and save the world.

My consciousness battled with me for a couple minutes. Could I kill someone though? Does a zombie still carry any part of their former human self? These thoughts didn't last long, as a flesh eater started to head straight for me. I dodged this one easily and ran back towards the hallway Matt and I came from.

As I made my way to the kitchen, I found it was no longer vacant—Mac was standing directly in front of the stove. I looked at him with dysphoria. There he was, the cause of all this really, and yet, I felt sadness instead of anger. His vacant expression while he searched for something to sink his teeth into looked so—so tragic. He was once a strong, authoritative man, only to be succumbed to this flesh-eating robot by his own hand.

As I stood their pitying him, I finally decided that while this all started with Mac, it would end with him too. I walked into the kitchen and ran to the freezer, propping it open as I stepped inside. I made my way to the back behind a shelf and generated as much noise as I could. Mac staggered in, catching my scent.

As soon as he was close enough, I pushed the shelf on top of him, and sprinted out, locking the door behind me. I grabbed the two extra propane tanks next to the walk in as I made my way over to the stove, but I realized something. How was I going to do this, and make it out alive?

This is where I'm at. I'm writing this, because I know what I have to do. I can't let these flesh-eating fucks spread and potentially destroy our Earth. I've already turned the propane on high, I can smell it leaking into the whole room. I'm pulling the match out of the packet in my hand and blowing this place the fuck up.

Word of advice, if you ever get a text message from an unknown number … don't reply.

Nanny

$\mathcal{E}$VERYONE HAS THAT ONE TERRIFYING nightmare from their childhood they still remember, but what happens when they find out that it was real?

When my brother James and I were growing up, our family lived in an old Victorian Style home located in Massachusetts. It was a beautiful tribute to the profound craftsmanship of the early twenties; picture a life size rustic dollhouse with an absolutely stunning part glazed, timber framed porch. It was also very

NANNY

secluded, with our nearest neighbor being maybe a mile away.

We would spend most of our days outside, in the treehouse our father built, as we made up stories of pirates and treasures. I was always Blackbeard while James would be Calico, we were the unstoppable duo of the high seas. There was a special hole in the middle of the tree where we would hide our stolen treasures. James had noticed it the very first day after the fort was built.

As exciting as our tree house was though, I would have to say the best part about our home was our Nanny. She was so thoughtful and fun, the best Nanny any child could ask for, really. During the rainy days, she would often sit with us in our room, telling us stories as she rocked in the chair. I'll admit, some were a little different than I had remembered.

For instance, when she would tell us the story about the little deer named Bambi, it wasn't the mother who had been killed. Instead, it was Bambi himself. She would always remind us that we needed to listen to our parents, so monsters like the hunters couldn't hurt us. She really did care.

At night, we would hear a soft humming sound that echoed throughout our whole room. It would lull us to sleep, enveloping our minds with such a calmness that we barely had any dreams, only that soft sweet hum from Nanny.

Some nights though, James and I would startle awake, both having had the same nightmare. Frequently it involved not being able to breathe, as if someone had placed a bag over our heads or shut off our air supply somehow. We would always wake up right before we died, hands on our throats, as we coughed away the night terror.

The mornings after these episodes, we would wake up to find Nanny had left us a note. We couldn't quite make out all the scribbles, but I was sure I caught the word "sorry." We always knew she wanted us to be happy and forget about the terrible shadows that haunted our minds.

We would often tell our parents about *Nanny*, and how she was so kind, leaving us notes in the night. They would usually comment on how feverish our imaginations were, also adding in how we needed to stop getting into the craft bin without asking. Honestly, I think they were just jealous that we were both so fond of Nanny, she had quickly become our favorite person over the years.

I remember the first time I brought a girl home. Her name was Gema and she had the cutest dimples. I was about fifteen years old at the time, just learning all the ins and outs of young love. I thought we were

NANNY

going to grow up and get married, and I wanted nothing more than Nanny's approval.

When her mother pulled up the driveway to drop her off, I couldn't contain my excitement. "Nanny, she's here!" I remember yelling, before I bounded out the door to greet Gema. As we made our way up the front steps, I half expected Nanny to be waiting for us just on the other side of the door, and when she wasn't, I grew worried.

I told Gema to wait in the kitchen for me while I went searching for her, but to my utmost disappointment, Nanny was nowhere to be found. The night dragged on after that, all I could think of was my dear friend. Why did she not want to meet Gema? Did she know something I didn't? Unfortunately, it left such a bad taste in my mouth, I never asked, and Gema was the last girl I ever brought home.

James and I eventually grew up and moved out of our family abode, leaving poor Nanny behind. We could feel her sadness as we packed our bags, on what would be our last night home. We both took the time to each write Nanny a goodbye letter that we placed on each of our nightstands, we knew she would appreciate that later.

We had got an apartment together in the city, and boy, was it different. We both received full rides to

Boston University, each taking on a different major. I had decided I wanted to be a teacher, while James was interested in Engineering, he was more interested in getting his hands dirty, I guess. The schoolwork was time-consuming, but we never forgot about Nanny.

Years later, I was going to write my college thesis on my childhood, and how I was basically raised by a Nanny. While looking up our family home, I stumbled across an article online, written about the original family that lived there in 1915. A mother and father, two little ones, and their nanny. Wait—*our* Nanny.

My head began to spin as I inspected the article more thoroughly. Was this really the same woman? How is that possible? I was confused, but I guess a little excited to learn all I could about the woman, or I guess spirit, who had helped raise both my brother and myself. I nostalgically thought to myself, maybe she missed the kiddos from the previous family and that's why she took such good care of us!

I could not have been more wrong.

The word "murderer," caught my eye and I quickly scanned further down the article, mortified at what I was reading. A lump began to form in the back of my throat, as my heart sank deep into my chest.

NANNY

The article reported how the Nanny had lost both of her children due to the negligence of a drunk driver in 1913. Never having been able to properly cope with their deaths, she actively searched for the monster that had stolen her babies' lives. That is when she became employed by the Dobson's.

On her journey for revenge, she had taken her time, caring for the monster's children as if they were her own. Until that dreadful night when she murdered the two sleeping babes. She had smothered them with a pillow, most likely singing to them ever so sweetly, as she always did.

After they had died, the article stated that the Nanny had written what appeared to be a suicide letter and left it next to their bodies. She then killed herself.

At the very bottom, was a photo of the backyard in which my brother and I used to play. In the middle, was the tree our fort had been built upon. As I looked closer, I noticed our treasure hole, only, it looked different. It was covered in a deep crimson red that made my own blood run cold.

Next to the tree was the lifeless body of our Nanny, *gun still in hand.*

Cold Blooded

$\mathcal{I}$ WOKE UP TODAY IN SOMEONE ELSE'S body in an unfamiliar bed. As I glanced around the room, I could see trophies shining back at me that were not my own. Honor awards posted on the wall. Pictures of friends and family that were like passing strangers on a full bus. I frantically ran to the bedroom mirror, only to see an African American teenager staring back at me. My heart began to frantically pound in my chest as I reached up and touched my unfamiliar face.

"Honey, are you almost ready to go? You're going to be late for school," I heard a woman yell from somewhere in the house.

COLD BLOODED

I looked around the room for anything familiar and noticed a backpack slouched over a chair, my backpack. I quickly ran to it only to be disappointed by the contents. These weren't my books, or any of my possessions. I sighed.

I put on the stranger's clothes and made my way out the door. I was immediately welcomed by the smell of fresh cooked bacon, something my mom frequently made for me in the morning as well. I rushed to the kitchen and was greeted by a woman eagerly cleaning up the morning mess.

"Oh great, you're up! Hungry?" she smiled as she handed me a plate stacked high with pancakes and bacon.

I nervously smiled back as I sat down. Given the circumstances I was anything but hungry, but just like my own mother, the woman smiled at me adoringly, waiting for me to dig in. As I was shoveling the delicious fluffy cakes into my mouth, I could hear the TV from the other room.

"RoPo! We are there because we care."

Laughter ensued behind me almost immediately. I stared up at the woman curiously, and she shook her head and sighed. "Didn't you hear? The last of the good, hardworking Police Officers quit last week. They were tired of being lumped in with RoPo."

Before I could ask what the hell a RoPo was, she turned back around to the dishes.

Once I was finished, she took my plate and swiftly kissed my forehead before telling me to have a good day at school and to please be safe. The last sentiment threw me off a bit, but I slung my backpack over my shoulder and headed out the door.

There was no way I was going to school.

I immediately took off running down the road trying to find any place that was familiar to me. As I passed the houses, I could see I was in a predominantly ethnic neighborhood, which being born a white male and what you hear on the news, it normally would have made me a little nervous. Today however, I was more scared of finding out what was going on than I was my surroundings.

As I was just about to reach the end of the block, I saw a boy about my age running with three of his friends. They all had a look of terror on their faces as they passed by me, "Hide, man! They're coming!" One of them shouted from behind.

The hairs on the back of my neck stood on end as I quickly came to a stop. I was just about to turn and follow them when I heard a gunshot, followed by a woman screaming. Everything in me wanted to run away from the sound, but that woman's scream beckoned me to follow. I rounded the corner in time to see a robot standing over the body of a young man lying on the pavement.

Its steel face showed no emotion as it stood there, hand still on the trigger of its gun. Red hollow sockets of light took the place where eyes should have been.

"They killed my baby!" a woman wailed as another robot held her back. I glanced down at the lifeless body of the teenager. He was wearing a backpack just like I was, probably on his way to school.

I overheard one of the robots whispering about a weapon. The one standing over the body held up his hand, as if to dismiss the silly claim that they would be blamed in any way. They were robots. Made in a factory void of all empathy and love; how could they make any mistakes?

On the verge of passing out from the rush of adrenaline, I reached for my stranger's phone to call for help. As my hand went to my back pocket, one of the robots jerked in my direction.

"Get down on the ground!" he yelled, pointing his gun right at me. Before I had the chance to respond I heard the sound of gunfire crack against my ear. My hands reflexively went to my stomach as the pain began to radiate through my body. I fell to the ground, head swimming from the blast.

As I laid there on the pavement, I thought of you. What your life would have been like had you gotten the chance to grow up. I thought of your mother and how her heart would break. I thought of what the news would say. Would they lie? Would they say you deserved it? Would they talk about your trophies? About how you were on the honor-roll at your school? Would any of it even matter?

A single tear fell from my face as I took your last breath. Then I woke up.

Animal Control

$\mathcal{I}$T HAD BEEN A LONG DAY OF GETTING terribly restless sleep. The sun was just beginning to set, which meant my shift would be starting soon. I groaned as my phone went off before my alarm. "Hello," I grumbled crankily into the speaker.

"Hey, Belle? Um. Pete says he needs you to get down to the shelter ASAP. Something's happened and well ... you're just gonna have to come see for yourself."

Wiping the sleep from my eyes I told my partner Benny I'd leave in five. Oh, the joys of being an Animal Control Officer on graveyard; we always get the weird shit. I swiftly got dressed, brushed my teeth, tossed my hair into a messy bun, and grabbed my vest as I rushed to the car.

Fuck, no coffee today. There's no time.

I pulled up to the shelter and could instantly tell something was wrong. My supervisor was pacing the front door, yelling irrationally into his phone. "I don't give a bear's behind, Jack, I said get down here now!" Jack is the Veterinarian for our local shelter. When he gets called in, you know it's bad.

I turned off the engine. Got one foot on the asphalt before I was bombarded by Benny.

"Thank God you're here, Belle. I've never seen anything like this, it's—it's terrible! Quick, follow me."

I passed my boss who was still red-faced, arguing with Jack. He gave me a worried glance as I opened the door. Benny was taking me to the kennels located at the far end of the building; that's where we kept the extreme cases. You know, the animals who want to kill you simply because you exist? So fun.

There was a distinct coppery taste in the air upon entering the isolation ward, along with the smell of Parvo. If you have smelled that, it's unforgettable.

We finally reached the furthest kennel and Benny stopped me before I could peek inside. "This. This isn't natural Belle. I don't know what, or who did this, but it's just … well, take a look," Benny motioned for me to go in.

I peered into the kennel and what I saw made my stomach churn. The animal, if you could even call it that, had been completely mutilated. I'm talking, its insides were now its outsides. It appeared to have been a Rottweiler at some point in its life; now it was just rot, decaying away in a kennel. Whatever had done this had to have been big, with a bite-force matching that of a crocodile.

I looked back at Benny. "Wh—who called this in?" I stuttered.

"It was anonymous; we picked him up on the outskirts of Bradley Park," he replied.

"Hmm, no collar. You think it was a stray?" I asked. "Any reports of missing pups matching his uh, well, what was his description?"

"Nope, none. My guess would be a 4-9 due to the lack of collar or microchip." Benny looked down at the mess of hair and viscera and shuddered.

We both made our way back to the front to figure out our next plan of attack. Our boss gave me a nod before retreating to his office. That meant we had the go ahead to find this beast, and we needed to find it now!

We promptly left the shelter and headed to my Jeep. I knew this was going to be a long night. "Where are we going to start?" whispered Benny. I looked at him with a sinister smile. "At the place where all things go to die … " Benny's face dropped. "Nah, I'm just fucking with you. let's go get some coffee, we're gonna need it."

Once we sucked down our bean juice, we headed to Bradley Park. Benny pointed to the spot where they had picked up the mangled mess. I parked the car as close to the scene as I could and hopped out, Benny at my tail. I bent down to look for prints when I spotted a large black shadow step back into the bushes to my left. I reached for my baton and signaled Benny to hover behind in case whatever it was made a run for it.

I inched forward, heart beating in my chest as I grabbed at the branches. I heard a low deep growl that sent shivers down my spine. I'm quite used to my job, and rarely does an animal strike fear into my bones anymore, but this … this was different. Due to the darkness the creature was encased in, I wasn't taking any chances.

I reached behind me to grab the restraining pole from Benny. I could tell he was shaking as he laid it in my hand. I positioned myself, ready for anything, and slowly stuck the pole further into the bush. Snap! The creature bit the pole in two before leaping towards me.

Standing inches from my face was the largest jet-black german shepherd I had ever seen in my entire life. We stood at a standstill, each waiting for the other to move. His lips pulled back into a snarl while his throat vibrated with intensity. I looked right into his eyes, not wanting to stand down, and that's when I noticed the golden metallic flecks. His bright green eyes were filled with them!

The beast's ears flew forward as he repositioned his shoulders. Almost as if he was taunting me. I began to stand taller when Benny gently touched my shoulder, causing me to jump. In that instant the shepherd bolted. I began the chase on foot while Benny ran for the Jeep.

I was right on the dog's tail all the way to the park bathrooms before I lost him. I turned around to see Benny quickly park the Jeep and run towards me. "Where did he go?" he shouted.

I put my finger to my lips. "I'm sure he couldn't have gone too far." I cranked my neck around the side of the building. No dog in sight, only a mangy tabby cat devouring a rat.

I sighed. "He's not here," I whispered.

Benny came around the corner and paused. He pointed down at the cat. "What is that?"

I looked down at the orange stray staring right at me with bright green eyes. No fucking way. I took a step forward and the cat arched its back, causing me to pause. I bent down, looking closer into the green marbles and saw them: the gold flecks.

As I looked at the rat, he had been devouring seconds earlier, I noticed it wasn't a rat at all. It was the shepherd. What was left of it, that is.

Once again, the chase was on. "What about the dog?" Benny called as he ran the opposite direction towards the Jeep.

"Forget the fucking dog!" I yelled back as I raced deeper into the park. I had tailed the creature to the north side of Bradley before it ran across a busy street and disappeared on the other side.

Out of breath I bent down, resting my hands on my knees as Benny pulled up next to me. I climbed in and reached for my water. "What is going on Belle? Why did that thing have such weird eyes?" Benny questioned. I glanced over at him. "I have no fucking idea, but we are going to find out."

We decided to head back to the shelter and talk to our boss; maybe he had some news for us. On the way, we got a call.

ANIMAL CONTROL

"Belle? Are you two by Abbey Street and Hampshire?" My boss's voice crackled through the stereo speakers.

"Well, we were on our way back to you. What's up?"

"Turn around and go back, we got a call. Someone's Chihuahua is trying to eat a neighbor kid. Sounds serious."

I rolled my eyes. A chihuahua? Really? "Alright sir, on our way." I ended the call.

Benny flipped a bitch and headed towards the cross streets. I wasn't sure we would know exactly which house to stop at until I saw the crowd. We quickly parked and ran towards the commotion. As we weaved through the hoard of people, a lady grabbed me.

"Are you Animal Control? Oh, thank God! My sweet Sophie was outside doing her nightly business when she got into a tiff with this ugly stray cat! The beast bit her and ran off!" she sobbed.

"I'm sorry to hear that ma'am," I said calmly. "We were told a child was in danger? Can you tell me where Sophie is now?"

The woman, now hysterical, pointed behind her house. Benny and I pushed through the crowd in the direction she pointed, passing a sobbing five-year-old along the way. Benny stopped to make sure she was okay as I kept walking. Once I reached the fence, I opened the connecting gate and squeezed my way in.

I heard the snarls before I even reached the pooch. I peeked around the house and immediately caught sight of the bright green eyes in the dark. I rounded the corner fully and faced the creature head on, slowly backing it into a corner. That's when it spoke.

"Leave me be or more will die," the small dog bellowed in a hauntingly demonic voice. His eyes started to turn red as he violently shook.

My mouth dropped open, stunned at what I was witnessing. The chihuahua's mouth stretched wide with rows of sharp pointy teeth as it let out a guttural screech that chilled my bones. It suddenly began chanting in a language I didn't understand, eyes locked on mine the whole time. I began to feel lightheaded as Benny rounded the corner. "I got him this time Belle!" he yelled as he launched towards the demon dog.

"Benny, n-."

I was too late.

He had wrapped the restraining pole around its tiny neck with such force, I thought it might snap. With no hesitation, he scooped up the hollering creature and stuffed it into the bag he had looped into his belt. "We got him!" Benny cried. I was still in too much shock to speak.

We headed back towards the crowd, Benny in the lead. I pulled myself together and walked over to Sophie's owner while Benny loaded up the pooch. "Sorry ma'am, we are going to have to take Sophie in and get her tested. This behavior isn't normal." I handed the sobbing woman my card and told her to call in the morning.

The ride back to the shelter was awkward. Benny excitedly talked for the whole twenty-minute ride about how proud our boss would be, while I sat in silence. I could hear the low growls from the back seat and shuddered. This was no ordinary dog, and this certainly was not an ordinary case. Ugh, how do I explain all this without sounding crazy.

When we reached the shelter, Benny jumped out and opened up the back. "Careful Benny, I—I'm not sure about this. Something seems off." I nervously pulled at my baby hairs as he grabbed the kennel.

"Oh, hush Belle, you are just mad you hesitated. Let me have this one," he chimed before heading in.

Benny walked right past our boss Pete, a pep in his step all the way to isolation. I shuffled over to him, scratching the back of my head. Oh, where to begin. I started to open my mouth when Jack angrily walked through the doors. "What's all this about Pete? You call me down here in the middle of the fucking night, it better be for a damn good reason." I looked at my boss, waiting for him to reply. Instead, he patted me on the shoulder and told me to fill Jack in.

I sighed. "Follow me." I led Jack towards the isolation room and ran into Benny halfway there. "She's all set up, and boy is she a feisty one," he announced. We took Jack to the far back kennels and first showed him the mutilated rottie. He pushed his glasses further onto his nose as if it would help the situation. It didn't.

"Whew, that one's a doozy. What did that?" he asked. I moved to the side and pointed at the snarling chihuahua in the kennel directly across from the heap of dog. "That did this? You've got to be shitting me," Jack announced.

Benny looked at me confused. I shook my head.

"Well, guess we better put the little beast down then huh? I'll go grab my bag. Also, what the hell is up with those eyes? I've never seen such a thing." Jack walked off towards the front and Benny turned to me. "What was that all about? I thought the shepherd killed him." I looked at my partner, not knowing where to start. Luckily, Jack returned before I had to.

ANIMAL CONTROL

Benny grabbed the restraining pole and got the loop around the thrashing chihuahua while Jack set up his supplies on the table outside of the room. "Be careful, Benny. Please, there's something really wrong with this one," I begged my partner. The dog stopped snarling and looked directly into my eyes, causing goosebumps to rise over my entire body.

Benny pulled the dog out of the kennel room all the way to Jack on the other side, and with precise restraint, he lifted the now completely still dog up onto the table. I walked around to the other side, ready to assist at any moment. My beeper went off in my pocket, letting me know there was a call coming in. It could wait.

Once Jack was all prepped, he slowly went to insert the needle into a vein. As he did so, I noticed the dog's eyes begin to shift color, from green to dark brown. I reached for Jack, but it was too late. The needle had been inserted and the pentobarbital had already begun to take effect.

Jack waited a few minutes before checking for a heartbeat. "That'll do it," he said. Once he was sure Sophie had passed, he gathered up his things, and Benny tagged and bagged the poor hound. Exhausted, I made my way towards the front, Benny and Jack following behind.

Not quite sure what to make of things, I sat down in the lobby to debrief myself while Jack and Benny talked to Pete. I couldn't quite understand what had just happened. Where did the demon go? Why was it even here? I had so many questions that I knew I would probably never receive the answers for. I just needed to let it go. This wasn't the first-time weird shit has happened during the night shift, and I doubted it would be the last.

"See ya around, Belle," Jack called as he exited the office.

Benny Trailed behind him. "Yeah, I think I'm gonna take off too; it's been a rough night," he yawned. As he gathered up his things, I noticed he was humming a tune I had never heard before. "Hey, where's that from? One of your animes?" I joked.

Benny turned around and smiled. "There's just some things you don't need to worry about Belle," he said with a twinkle in his green eyes. "You have a good night now, and I'll be seeing you very soon."

I sighed. "Yeah, you too, Benny." I started to make my way towards the office when Benny's bag caught my eye; he had forgotten it. I rushed out to the parking lot to stop him, but he was already gone.

ANIMAL CONTROL

That's when a thought crossed my mind that made my heart sink deep into my chest. Benny has brown eyes.

Don't Forget to Breathe

𝓗AVE YOU EVER SAT THERE AND wondered what would happen if your brain forgot to tell your lungs to breathe?

Inhale.

Exhale.

Inhale again.

You are probably feeling it now. Feels weird, doesn't it?

The more you think about it, the more your natural rhythm seems off. Is this how you normally breathe? What if it isn't? Do you control your breathing? If not, who does?

It's like when you say a word over and over in your head. It starts to lose its meaning and almost sounds foreign in a way. Where did that word even come from? Your brain starts to wonder if you made it up all along.

At least, that's what they want you to think.

I learned a long time ago that when you start to question how your mind works, they send you triggers. Your pulse will rise. Confusion sets in. The world you know seems to fall apart at the seams until finally, finally your brain resets.

You probably notice your heart beating a little faster now that I have told you, huh? Mine too, but don't worry, things will all go back to normal soon enough.

Do you feel that itch though? Feels like a spider is crawling over your body. It's tiny little legs gently caressing your skin, making it a home, burrowing deeper and deeper.

Ignore it.

That's your brain distracting you from what I'm about to say. Diverting your attention to something else.

It usually happens before you fall asleep. If you lay still for a while, eyes closed, just before your mind gives way to your dreams, you will feel the tingle. It's normal, happens to everyone, but when you stay awake and ignore it … well, that's when things start to get scary.

You see, your brain sends out the signal to check if you are still awake. If you are, your hand will instinctively swat at the sensation, letting them know it's not safe. If you are asleep, that's when they will come.

They will first immobilize you. Ever hear of sleep paralysis? What if I told you that happens whether you are awake or not? Every single night.

They have to make sure you are completely still so no mistakes are made. You think your dreams are random? Guess again. They create them for you as a distraction to ensure you don't wake up, unless … unless you never really fell asleep. Then you will see them.

The shadow people, as I like to call them. Dark figures without faces that control how we live. Some like to think of them as their subconscious, but I've seen them, and I can tell you, they are very real.

Nothing you do is your choice, it's theirs. If you start to doubt yourself and the way things are, they will correct it, but not before releasing anxiety to stop it from happening again. They have programmed our brains to do that.

You are probably feeling anxious right now, and I'm sorry for causing it, but you needed to know. Don't fall asleep tonight. Stay awake. Fight the itch. Fight the urge to let your mind wander, and you will see. You will see the shadows; you will know that I was telling the truth.

And then you will wake up.

Unless they make sure you forget how to.

Arachnophobia

𝓐RE YOU AFRAID OF SPIDERS? WELL, YOU should be. Some people say that they help us more than they harm us, but I don't believe that to be true. If someone were to break into your house at night but also watered all of your plants, would it make it okay? For me, that answer is no.

Yes, tell them.

Last night I saw one above my bed. It stared down at me with its millions of beady little eyes, watching. Waiting. I made a quick dash for the flyswatter I keep on my nightstand and it followed me. Moving its body along with mine, it was taunting me.

I steadied myself up onto my shaking legs while goosebumps spread throughout my body as if tiny

ARACHNOPHOBIA

little spider legs were caressing my skin. The enemy jerked in my direction and we were at a standstill.

I took a deep breath and pulled the flyswatter back, ready to launch.

I missed. The spider was gone.

My whole body began to itch as I imagined it crawling underneath my clothes. With my arms flailing violently, I danced on my bed, shaking everything off in the process.

Silly human.

That's when I felt it, sneaking its way inside of my ear. I screamed as my hand frantically tried to grab hold of the invader. I was too late. I could feel it make its way deeper inside of my head and I wanted to die.

That's when I heard the voice.

Are you afraid of spiders? Well, you should be.

The Florist

I AM A WEDDING FLORIST, AND HAVE been for quite some time now. I specialize in exotic flowers that no one around town has ever come close to replicating, making my business one of a kind.

Sometimes, if I am feeling extra sentimental, I'll bring my beauties to the wedding myself. I adore the atmosphere that new love creates; two souls forever finding their eternal resting place in one another. I wish I could have experienced it for myself.

Just two weeks before my big day, I caught my fiancé Brad in our basement with my best friend Katie. They were doing much more than just refilling their wine glasses. I was heartbroken and vowed to never fall in love again.

THE FLORIST

I kicked Brad out of our house that we had made a home and told Katie she could keep the lying bastard. I didn't hear from them again for years—until yesterday.

I had opened up my email to find a message from Brad himself. He actually had the audacity to tell me that him and Katie were going to get married, and that he would love nothing more than for me to be their florist.

My whole body began to tremble. I could feel the icicles of my cold, dead heart shatter with each anger induced beat. I pushed my laptop away from me in disgust. *How the hell could he ask me such a thing?* I ran to the liquor cabinet and rage drank the thought of Katie in a white gown from my mind.

I woke up this morning with a hangover from hell banging on my head. *"Knock, knock guess who's getting married. Surprise! It's Katie, not you."* my subconscious mocked. I groaned and reached for my laptop.

As I opened it up, fully prepared to give him a giant finger for a reply, something caught my eye. In the right-hand corner of the screen there was an ad for rare flowers. My curiosity got the better of me and I clicked it, Brad could wait.

My screen instantly became filled with gigantic species of Sarracenia. Have you ever heard of the plants that can eat a whole mouse? Picture those, only the size of a small tree. Intrigued, I began scrolling until I saw a vibrant purple one with rose gold petals, it was beautiful. The description said it was called Marriage Noir, how fitting.

I scrolled back up to the top of the page and hit info:

> *Hello, welcome to Sinister Seedlings. Do you have a problem with a boss that is too touchy? Maybe a cheating Hubby? How about a frenemy that you can no longer fake a smile with? Well, we can help with that! Our seedlings are the cream of the crop and promised to fulfill all of your darkest desires. All you need to do is add water and watch them grow in just two months' time. Once matured, give our little devils to the person of your choosing and watch the magic happen.*

A terrible feeling arose in the pit of my stomach. Who would make such a flower? Better yet, who would *buy* one? I felt disgusted.

I opened back up Brad's message and searched for the wedding date. July 4th, how cliche. I began to write out a heartfelt response back to him and my horrible excuse of a friend. I told them that I was terribly sorry and that I was all booked up for the summer. I added in that I would however, love to come to their wedding and support them. I was actually kind of happy that he contacted me. It was time to let bygones be bygones.

I hit send and quickly clicked over to Sinister Seedlings. I scrolled all the way down to Marriage Noir and clicked buy. Afterall, purple *was* Katie's favorite color, and who shows up to a wedding empty handed?

It Was Always Meredith's Fault

I KNOW FOR THOSE OF YOU WHO HAVE daughters, you have probably heard about American Girl dolls a time or two. Those of you who haven't, let me explain. American Girl dolls are lifelike little humans that every crotch fruit just has to have. They are also every parent's wallet's worst nightmare.

My daughter Lilith turned four last month. On her birthday list was just one thing, you guessed it, one of those dolls. I had searched online for days to see if maybe I could grab some sort of deal, when an ad popped up on one of the sites: *Don't want to pay full price for an American Girl doll? You don't have to. Click here.*

IT WAS ALWAYS MEREDITH'S FAULT

I practically jumped in my seat at the opportunity! The website seemed legit and the dolls looked almost identical to the real thing, only *half* the price. I scrolled through until I found the perfect one; a blonde doll with tight curls, bright blue eyes, and adorable freckled cheeks that mimicked my Lilith perfectly.

I immediately placed her in my shopping cart along with some outfits and continued with the order, Lil was going to be so excited!

It took about a week for the doll to arrive, which was right on time for the party. When Lilith opened up the bright pink package, she was ecstatic! "Thank you, thank you, thank you, Mama!" she screamed, and just like that, I felt like a hero.

Lilith had promptly given her the name Meredith, and she went *everywhere* with her, even the bathtub. I didn't mind at first, I remembered my favorite doll from when I was younger. Her name was Gracie. My mom had found her at an estate sale, already named in a sweet little box. I was so heartbroken when I lost her.

About two weeks after Lilith's birthday however, her attitude started to change. She had always been a well-behaved child; picked up her toys when asked, used her manners regularly, and always had a smile on her face, that is, before Meredith arrived.

Every morning I would find Lil's room a complete disaster, and every morning I would receive the same excuse: Meredith did it. I had also found her favorite teddy bear, from when she was a baby, in the oven one day. That was Meredith's fault too apparently.

Being pregnant with my second child, I was under a lot of stress. Maybe Lilith was acting out due to the eventual change that was about to occur in our lives. Sometimes she would bring Meredith over to my stomach to let her listen, sweetly humming a song as she did. Repeating the words "soon, very soon."

As the days went on though, my little girl became severely withdrawn, only wanting to spend time with Meredith. Some nights I could hear Lil talking to her for hours in her bed, almost as if she was replying.

I really started to become concerned when I tried to take Meredith away. My sweet little darling panicked. "You can't take her, Kate! She'll kill you!" She screamed. I stood there with my mouth dropped to the floor and slowly handed her back to my frantic daughter. She had never called me by my name before.

That night, after Lilith had gone to bed, I went online to check out the website. I quickly typed in the URL, hit enter, and my blood ran cold.

Error, page not found.

IT WAS ALWAYS MEREDITH'S FAULT

Frustrated, I shut down the computer and snuck into my daughters' room. Meredith was tightly snuggled into her arms, staring up at me with a slight smirk on her freckled face. I'm not sure why, but a haunting chill ran through my body just from that glance. As I turned to walk back out, I thought I heard a giggle, but as I glanced at Lil, she was peacefully asleep. I shook my head and closed the door behind me.

A couple days later, the nightmares began. I would startle awake, sweat pouring from my face as visions of Lilith with a knife flashed through my mind. Only, in my dream it wasn't really her. It was a sinister version of her. A Meredith version. Just before she plunged the knife into my stomach, she would whisper, "She's ready to be born now." Same dream. Every night for a week.

This brings us to yesterday. About an hour after I had tucked her in, my daughter came into my room crying. Through her sobs, she told me that Meredith had hurt her hamster. With a sinking feeling in the pit of my stomach, I raced to her room. My heart sank into my chest when I saw MC Hammy, laying lifeless in Meredith's lap.

I turned around to my now hysterical daughter.

"Why Lilith? Why would you do this?" I screamed.

"I … I didn't mama, I t—told you, it was Meredith." she sobbed. I bent down to her level as my eyes began to swell with tears.

"Meredith is *just* a doll, Lilith! She can't do these kinds of things. She's just a doll!" I said with worry on my tongue. Lil looked up at me confused.

"Then why do her eyes move, mommy?"

I stared at my daughter; words caught in my throat as I struggled to find the right ones. I pulled her into a hug, already mentally preparing all her future counseling sessions, when I glanced up at the mirror behind her.

Just in time to see Meredith wink.

Love, The Easter Bunny

$\mathcal{L}$AST EASTER, MY SON, GRANT, DECIDED

he was going to find the Easter Bunny. The night before had been a rough one and we didn't have time to do our yearly routine of reading "Mr. Bunny," and leaving carrots out. He was pretty upset, but we managed.

Grant woke up at dawn, put on his raincoat and boots and eagerly ran out the door, basket in hand. My husband and I took the opportunity to quickly scatter all of his eggs in the backyard while he was distracted, it was perfect.

We were only gone for about five minutes before we excitedly walked around to the front yard to check on his progress. He wasn't there. I remember my husband making a game of it and whispering, "hmm I wonder where little G is," but after about the fifth time of guessing wrong, we started to worry.

We knocked on neighbor's doors, checked inside the house to see if maybe he snuck back in, everywhere. He was just gone. We immediately called the police and filed a report. Weeks turned into months, posters began to fade on the poles they rested on, and Amber Alerts slowly died down—along with our hopes.

We never fully recovered. My husband turned into an alcoholic and lost his job. I became so depressed and withdrawn from the world, that I needed to be heavily medicated. I think the "not knowing what happened," is what really got to me. Who took my baby? Was he okay?

The whole year was a complete blur to me. I missed my baby. I would have given anything to have him in my arms again, to take back the silly argument we had the night before he vanished. Was it really that difficult to take some extra time before bed to make him happy?

Unfortunately, all of my questions were answered this morning.

LOVE, THE EASTER BUNNY

After a late night of binge drinking and crying over the year lost without our son, I was disappointed to be abruptly awoken by our doorbell chiming off its hinge. I groaned and pulled on my robe before making my way down the stairs.

I looked through our peephole and found no one on the other side of the door. Confused, I slowly pulled it open and peered through the crack I had created. Still no one. "Damn kids and their stupid pranks," I mumbled.

I was about to close the door when I caught site of a basket resting on the ground. My heart began to pound in my ears as I saw the frilly pastel colors taunting my shattered heart. I slowly bent down to pick it up, hands shaking rapidly, when I recognized Grant's rain boots.

Tears began to fall from my already swollen eyes. I eagerly picked up my baby's boots and with blurred vision, I noticed the note delicately placed inside of them. I snatched it out and opened it up, fingers still trembling. As I read the sloppy scribble on the inside, I crumbled to the floor.

Next time, don't forget the carrots.

My Biggest Fan

At THE AGE OF FOUR, MY PARENTS HAD enrolled me into piano lessons. They wanted me to have a hobby that would not only enrich my personal skills but would also give me an outlet later on in life. As I was an introvert by nature, they could not have introduced me to a better avocation.

I loved playing. My mind could relax as my hands slowly turned my inner thoughts into a sweet lullaby. The songs could execute my feelings flawlessly into a language only I understood, making it the only time I ever felt truly heard.

I often played alone in my bedroom, appreciating the solitude it granted me. My own musical sanctuary that would shield me from the terrifying force known as socialization.

No matter how deep I was immersed in my seclusion, I would still be greeted by the sound of my parent's applause after each forte. It gave me such a sense of pride and accomplishment as my heart swelled, something one can only gain from hard work and dedication.

As I grew older, my song style began to change, forming into my own tune. Some would compare me to a modern Chopin. His rendition of Nocturne, as beautifully haunting as it was, speaks to my tormented soul on an unexplainable level.

Without fail, my parents continued to support me. No matter how dark my musical tastes became, I could still hear their claps of adoration of my art. It was their love and support that paved the way for me to eventually accept a full ride scholarship to the top musical arts college in the country.

The weekend before my first day of school, I packed up my things and prepared myself for the new adventure. I traced my fingers along the biographies encased upon my bookshelf: Stravinsky, Penderecki, and Bartok, all huge influences on my musical career.

Upon finishing, and feeling rather emotional, I decided to play just one last time on my first piano. I needed a cathartic release of this chapter, before embarking on what would be my biggest adult endeavor.

I picked a special aria, one that truly spoke to the essence of my heart: Chopin's 2nd Ballad. It was a perfect way to end the funeral for my youth. When the song was done, I could hear the clapping once more. Pride filled my chest, as tears welled up in my eyes. I was going to miss my parents so much.

The next morning, I woke up to find a note sitting next to my bed. "I will always be with you," it read. Oh mom, she knew my love language so well. Around noon, we all packed into the car and headed out to what would be my new home for the next four years. I placed all my compositions on my bookshelf methodically, choking back tears as my parents set up the bed for me.

When everything was in its proper *new* place, my parents gave me a kiss and wished me luck. My mother had tears in her eyes as they left, my father's arm wrapped snugly around her waist in comfort. I quickly called out, "you will always be with me, remember?" My mother gave me a smile before blowing a kiss from the end of the hall.

I shut the door and sighed, alone once again, but in a new fortress of seclusion. I sat down and glanced over at the keyboard propped up on my desk. I smiled, what better way to christen the place than by

MY BIGGEST FAN

song. I played the very first melody I had ever written, with sweet tears staining my cheeks and the keys below the whole emotional time.

When I had finished, I was surprised to hear my parents' ovation. I walked over to my front door and opened it, expecting to see them lingering just a little longer, maybe waiting for one last hug.

The hall was empty.

Confused, I closed the door and walked back to the couch, eventually deciding to call my mom and tell her what had happened. I could practically hear her beaming through the phone. "That's because you are a magnificent musician my dear," she replied.

I sighed, thanking her for the compliment. As I brought up the fact that it reminded me of her and my father always cheering me on through the door of my angsty teen years, I heard the line go silent.

My mom spoke nervously, "What do you mean cheering you on *through* the door, honey?"

"Oh, you know, after every song I played while barricaded in my room, you and dad would clap for me from the other side. It was super encouraging," I replied.

"Sweetie," my mom gently replied, "your dad and I never really got to hear you play, other than at your recitals, of course. I wish you would have let us!"

My heart began to thud rapidly in my chest. Was I *that* vain that I heard my own personal applause every time I played? I nervously laughed and told my mom I would call her later. Upon hanging up, I brought my trembling hands back to my keyboard.

I shakily played an original song, heart racing as I knew I was approaching the end. When I was finished, a familiar sound made my skin crawl. Right next to my ear, as if someone was standing right beside me, I heard it …

… *My biggest fan's round of applause.*

I'm Turning into a Bee

My name is Seros, and I am turning into a bee.

When I was three years old, I was stung by my first winged floof. I was playing in the park, picking flowers like most three-year-old's do and *ouch!* One had a stinger. I remember running to my mom crying, holding my hand up to her as the swelling began to take over my tiny finger. Little did I know; mother's kiss wouldn't fix it this time.

By the time we got home, I knew I was different. I felt different. I walked into the kitchen and a strange sense of urgency flooded over my entire body. *Flowers.*

I need to find a flower. My eyes scanned the room quickly before I homed in on my target. The bouquet of tulips my mother had set near the window.

I skipped over to them, inspecting them carefully before shoving one into my mouth. The taste was indescribable. I shoveled four more in by the time my mother caught me. I'll never forget the look on her face as I smiled, petals hanging from my teeth.

The next time I would be stung was when I turned thirteen. I was out at my best friend's farm, helping bale some hay when Beenedict Stingerbatch got me. *How did I know his name?*

I yelped it pain as my friend rushed over. "Oh, it was just a bee mate, you'll be ok," he said. He couldn't have been more wrong.

When I got home that evening, I had a strange lump that had formed in the middle of my lower back. I rushed to the bathroom to investigate. As I looked in the mirror and scratched the strange new lump, *out popped a stinger!*

I instantly heard evil buzzing laughter ensue from outside the window. I slowly opened the blinds to a swarm of bees. My eyes widened as my body began to vibrate. What was happening to me? I pulled the blinds back down and quickly ran to my bedroom.

I'M TURNING INTO A BEE

It took hours before I could finally fall asleep. The next day I woke up and instantly reached for my stinger, it was still there. I sighed as I got up to go fetch a Band-Aid. On my way to the bathroom I was stopped by Honey Beeswax herself. She gently fluttered over to my shoulder and began to crawl up towards my ear.

Frozen in shock, I held my breath as I heard a tiny buzz like whisper escape her furry mouth.

Just one more sting and you can join the hive.

I shuttered and before I knew it she had lowered her poisonous derrière dart into my ear. I screamed, grabbing for my phone on the way down to the floor. I can feel my body changing, I only have a few minutes to get this out. *Ouch. Are those wing—zzzzzzzz.*

Gravity Hill

THERE IS A SECRET PLACE IN MY TOWN called Gravity Hill. The legend states that many, many years ago a school bus filled with children went over the edge just before it reached the top. The bus driver had been drinking. Supposedly, if you visit this hill and park your car in neutral at the bottom, it will begin to roll upwards.

Many people believe it is the children that push your car, attempting to get you to safety, so you don't have to endure the same fate they did. Some even say if you place talcum powder on your bumper, little fingerprints will be left after the ascent. I however, being a person of science, figured it was just one of those magnetic pull phenomena's, easily explained with a little bit of research.

Last week, a couple of friends and I decided to test this theory. We all loaded up in my car, talcum powder in hand, and set out on our journey.

Once we arrived you could feel the excitement in the air. Just because you don't believe in spirits possessing the ability to move your car, doesn't mean you can't enjoy the mysteries of the unknown.

Charlie got out and quickly sprinkled the white powder on the bumper, gave the trunk a little pat to let us know it was a go, and stepped back to record.

John and I squirmed in our seats in anticipation. One minute passed, five minutes passed, ten minutes passed. I turned to John with a half look of disappointment and another half of, "I told you so."

Then, the car started moving.

I inhaled sharply and looked over at my friend who had a wicked grin proudly displayed on his smug face. It took approximately five minutes to reach the top, apparently little kids can't push very fast.

Do I smell alcohol?

Once we reached the summit, the car began to swerve and slowly rock to the edge. John looked at me horrified. It was swerving with so much force it was almost as if I was intoxicated. I slammed my foot on the break, put the car in park and we both quickly jumped out and ran to the sides.

"What the hell was that?" John shouted.

I stared at my car, trying to find an explanation, as Charlie ran up to us out of breath. "What happened? Why were you guys swerving?"

Not wanted to seem like a child, I pulled myself together.

"I told you, it's got to be a magnetic pull or something, maybe this area is really close to the equator, I don't know. Magnets are unpredictable," I shrugged.

John looked at me with betrayal in his eyes as he slowly walked closer to the car. He glanced at the bumper and sighed. The talcum powder had been untouched.

"Yeah, I guess," he replied, still unsure, but also not wanting to show he was actually afraid.

Confused and feeling a bit let down, we all got back in the car and drove home. I dropped off Charlie first, waved goodbye and set out to John's house. He was the most disappointed. The ride was silent as he sulked. Once we reached his place, he gave me a look of "yeah, yeah, let it go," and hopped out of the car.

As soon as he shut the door, something caught my eye. I glanced into the back seat and noticed the light reflecting on the window. There were tiny handprints all over.

"No fucking way," I said out loud as I opened my car door. I walked around to the side of the car and looked closer. Sure enough, there *were* tiny child-like handprints all over both of my back windows.

I stood there dumbfounded; how did we miss these. I pulled my hoodie up over my hand and tried to clean them off, they didn't even smudge. I opened the back door and climbed in to get a closer look. Reaching for the window, I gave it a quick swipe.

My blood ran cold. The fingerprints weren't on the outside after all, they were on the *inside*.

Sweet Tooth

$\mathcal{F}$OR AS LONG AS I CAN REMEMBER, MY town has been terrorized by tourists, and the monster. Starting at a very young age, we are taught just two simple rules; avoid sweets—as it will entice the beast, and do not make friends with any visitors—as they can be deceiving. While most of us heed this advice with great care, others would pay for their rebellions.

Take Tommy Jameson for instance. He was never one to listen to our elder's warnings, always telling us that they used this idea of a monster, to make us behave and eat properly. I'll admit, it made a lot of sense, until the day Tommy brought a pack of donuts to class. He sat all the way in the back during our morning lecture, stuffing his face with the delicious jam fill desserts, as we all watched in horror.

He extended one of his powdered covered sins to Stacey, who promptly shot him a disapproving glance, before turning her back to him as she faced the front. Our teacher Ms. Raine however, occasionally gazed upon him with a fervent smile as she continued her lecture; she never did care for him too much.

When class had finished, Ms. Raine asked Tommy to stay behind. We could all feel the tension as we made our way towards the door to our lockers. I held my breath as I inched forward in line, taking one last glance at Tommy's arrogant expression, before Ms. Raine closed the door behind me. I had a bad feeling that would be the last time I saw him.

Without much surprise on my end, the next morning Ms. Raine told us that Tommy had been expelled due to his disruptive behavior, but we all knew the truth. He had broken a rule, and when rules get broken, people get hurt.

Our suspicions were confirmed when his body was found in the woods later that week. Well, what was left of it anyway. He had been violently ripped apart limb from limb with all of his vital organs missing—his parents were distraught; how could he be so careless?

The elders in our town would hold weekly meetings, especially after a death. I assume, discussing how to contain the monster from attacking one of our own. At one meeting they even discussed removing sweets from every shop in town, they were unsuccessful. Apparently, tourists just love to indulge in junk food while on vacation.

As years went by, more people disappeared; some of them never having been reported, as it was all part of living in this God forsaken town. Even still, no one ever seemed to move away, almost as if we were all stuck here upon being born.

When I reached the age of thirteen, I had my first run in with the monster. I was walking home from class, when a visitor approached me, asking for directions to the nearest shopping mall.

She was absolutely beautiful, with long amber hair that glowed when the sun touched it. Her voice serenaded me in song as she repeated her question. I was hypnotized. My heart began thudding rapidly in my chest as she inched closer, and then it hit me, like a cool breeze on a hot summer's day. The sickly-sweet smell enveloped my whole body, leaving me stiff as a board, yet begging me to follow her every move.

The woman stared at me with deep emerald eyes, enticing me, drawing me in. I took another deep inhale of her sweet scent before snapping back into reality. Adrenaline began coursing through my veins, I knew what she was, my parents had warned me about the monster's tricks. The beast came in all disguises, that's how it traps you, with its only tell being the redolence it gives off before it attacks. *Always avoid the tourists*

I stumbled backwards, waving my arms out in front of me as I begged for it to stop. Pleading for my life. The "woman" appeared frightened at first, then stared at me with betrayal in her eyes, she bolted back towards the town. I quickly jumped to my feet, running in the other direction, never stopping to see if she had followed.

As I reached my house, I bounded through the front door, causing my mother to drop the plate she had been washing. Out of breath, I struggled to explain my close call with the monster, as she yelled for my father. He came around the corner, surprise on his face, as he caught sight of my frightened expressions and trembling body.

My mother glanced at him with worried eyes as my father placed his hand on my shoulder. "I think you are old enough now, son," he said, beckoning me to follow him to the kitchen table. Once we sat down, my father told me the ugly truth about our town, and the ominous monster that has, and always will torment those who live here.

From that day forward, I was more terrified of the awful beast than I had ever been. Every tourist caused my body to tremble with anticipating desire. The scariest part; I have no preference, they all smell the same to me, all giving off the sickly-sweet scent that makes my mouth water. All the while, the monster is there, taunting me with three simple words over and over inside of my head—*just one taste.*

You Can Never Be Too Careful

ARE ANY OF YOU PARENTS? IF YOU ARE, I'M sure you will understand where I am coming from when I say that the playground is my favorite place to be! It's my time to think really, as the kiddos burn off all the built-up energy from the day.

Some parents might have a nanny who takes their kid to the park for them, and I think that's just lazy. If you don't have time for your children, you probably shouldn't have them. Others would kill for that time, I know I would, which is why I'm always here.

Rachel is about 4 years old and she seems to really enjoy the slides. She gets so excited when she arrives, running to the biggest one first, pigtails soaring behind her as she goes—what a fun age. I should really look into getting a small one for the playroom.

Her brother Robbie is close to 6 and he spends most of his time on the swings. I remember really enjoying the swings myself as a child, going higher and higher before jumping off. Closest thing to flying a child can get, I suppose.

Today I decided to bring a book with me while they played, not that I'd actually read it though, you can never be too careful. Just a few months ago, a child was taken from a playground down the street. His terrible excuse of a mother was far to busy on her phone. She simply didn't see him happily skip away with someone who had the time and attention he needed.

Book in hand, I watched Rachel and Robbie play a game of tag. Oh, how they loved to run. I reflexively turned a page, not having read a single line, as a woman sat down next to me. I looked over at her, giving a shy smile, as I noticed she was watching Rachel a little too intently. Goosebumps raised over my entire body.

Given the most recent events, this did not sit too well with me. A sickening feeling began to form in the deepest parts of my stomach, as adrenaline coursed through my veins. I sat my book down to my right as

YOU CAN NEVER BE TOO CAREFUL

I scanned the rest of the playground for more children.

I spotted two more kiddos who appeared to be around seven or nine, were their parents here too? Were they protected? I looked at the other benches around the park, empty. Those kids were alone. My eyes shifted back to the woman sitting next to me when I noticed she was staring right at me.

My heart began to race.

The woman saw me shift awkwardly and decided to break the silence. "Which one is yours?" She asked sweetly.

I ignored her.

Fortunately, she took the hint and swiftly moved to another bench. I released the breath I had been holding, and as I picked my book back up, I smiled. I swear I'm not a rude person, I just don't know the polite way to tell someone …

I haven't decided yet.

Cake

I USED TO LOVE CAKE; I REALLY DID—THE creamy, moist center, the buttery frosting, all of it. I wasn't prejudice when it came to the flavor of the delicate dessert either, well, that is until Samantha had to go and ruin everything.

We were both seventeen years old at the time, just getting ready to spread our adult wings. Sam couldn't have been happier, as she had a very troubled home life. Her parents had died in a car crash when she was just five years old, leaving her to live with her grandfather—he was a wretched old man.

The dinosaur was a two pack a day smoker, causing him to be hooked to an oxygen tank by the age of 45. Not that it stopped him from smoking, the idiot would take a few drags of his cancer stick, replace it with his oxygen mask for a few breaths, and then continue to kill himself—one puff at a time.

He treated Sam like complete dirt. Always yelling at her in his old smoker voice.

"Sam, bring me my glasses."

"Sam, bring me my slippers."

"Sam, come wipe my ass…"

Just the thought of it makes me cringe.

She told me about the first day she came to live with him. He hadn't yet been wheelchair bound and stood at about 6 feet tall—in the eyes of a five-year-old, he was a giant. His first words to her upon entering were, "don't worry kiddo, I'll teach you how to drive properly so you don't go and kill yourself like your idiot parents." She spent the rest of the day in her room.

Things only got worse for her throughout the years.

Sometimes his buddies would come over for poker nights and they would all take their turn tormenting Sam. "Accidentally" snubbing cigarettes on her arms as she brought them food, tripping her as she handed them their beers, some of them even made perverted advances as she grew older. All the while, her grandfather stared at her as if she was his annoying pet, laughing alongside his scumbag friends.

When she didn't feel like obeying his strict rules, she was struck by a wooden stick he kept on his person at all times. The punishments had caused permanent marks all over her body, deep embedded wounds. Over the years though, it was the mental abuse that really took a toll, and my friend began to mentally deteriorate.

She would start each day being told she was a nobody, she would be going nowhere in life, and no man would ever love someone so hideous—spit flying out his mouth as her verbally assaulted her spirit.

I wanted to get her help, begged her even. She would always object, apparently a foster home would have been worse. I still don't know how she hid it all from our teachers.

One day, while Sam and I were studying for a final exam, we heard her grandfather choke out, "Sam, I need my pills, now!" Sam sighed, looking at me with hate in her eyes and said, "I can't wait until the day he dies, I really can't", as she walked from her room to tend to him. I didn't blame her of course, I almost wished he would die too.

CAKE

Weeks passed and it was the old man's birthday. I had told Sam I would stay over to keep her company, as I knew what the night would entail. Every birthday since grandfucker had "cared" for her, he had made the day horrible—guilt tripping her if she wasn't at his beck and call at all times.

We were up in her room when we heard him yell, "Sammy, it's my birthday, I need my cake!"

This time Sam had decided to ignore him. She placed her headphones on top of her head, turning up her Walkman. Again, the bastard yelled.

"Sam! I said bring me my cake!!" Pounding his fists on the table as he roared. He had gotten much worse since the wheelchair.

Having heard him through her music, she began to shake with anger. I looked over at her with sympathetic eyes and what I saw in return terrified me. Sam had snapped. Reaching her breaking point, she ripped off her headphones and stood up, fists at her side.

Before I had a chance to calm her down, she stormed out of her room, bolting down the stairs with heavy steps as she went.

I heard her grandfather say, "It's about damn time you lazy cunt." There was no reply from Sam as I heard her exit the kitchen, to the attached garage. Moments later, I heard her come back in.

"What do you think you are doing?" Her grandfather asked. I could hear Sam wheeling him out to the garage before slamming the door behind her. There was a brief struggle and then—

Silence.

Minutes passed and I head a chainsaw start up as her grandfather began to yell. Have you ever heard the sound of flesh being torn apart? Well, I can now say that I have. I rushed down the stairs toward the garage, heart beating deep in my chest as I reached the door handle.

Locked.

I began pounding on the door, pleading with Sam to stop.

"Oh, grandfather, you are making such a mess, guess I'll be cleaning up after you yet again," I heard her say. What was she doing to him? I heard gurgling sounds before a hefty crunch.

"Pop goes the weasel," she sang light heartedly. More ripping sounds, then, silence again as she turned off the chainsaw. "Just gotta get this on top and … *crunch, crunch*, perfect! Oh, grandfather you look exquisite!"

Ten minutes had passed before I worked up the courage to speak again.

CAKE

"Sam? Sam please open the door, let me get you some help. We can figure this out, I promise," I begged her. I heard the door slowly unlock and I took a step back. As it opened, I held my breath. I noticed Sam had her back turned to me as she exited the garage, she was carrying something.

When she turned around my stomach churned as all the color washed from my face. Sam just stared at me, eyes beaming with appreciation for her work.

She approached me, platter in hand, grinning from ear to ear. Resting methodically on top was her grandfather's severed head. His eyes were wide with shock as his mouth lay open in horror. A makeshift "candle" appeared to have been hammered onto the top. I peered behind her at the gory scene that was displayed all over the garage, my expression matching her grandfathers.

Sam let out a small giggle as she placed his head onto the table.

"Would you like a slice of cake honey?" she purred.

While humming "Happy Birthday," she reached for the largest knife on the block and I slowly backed my way to the front door, dialing 911 in my pocket as I went. I guess the police found her in the kitchen twenty minutes later, chewing on a piece of his cheek, still humming that God-awful tune.

A week went by before I found out she had been taken to a psychiatric hospital, where she would spend the rest of her days. I have visited my friend twice in the last twenty years and I can tell you, to this day, she still wears a permanent grin on her unforgiving face. I, however, have never been able to look at a cake the same way.

Past Lives

I DIED MANY YEARS AGO. IT WASN'T THE first time, and it certainly won't be the last. I had made it to eighty-three before I left behind my legacy of children, grandchildren, and a sassy old cat that I still do not miss. My husband Frank, a gentle man and kindred spirit, died about six years before I did; I hope his new life has been treating him well.

Seconds after my last breath on Earth, I took my very next in The Cinema. I looked around at all my past lives with fond memories; they all smiled in return. As I nestled into my seat, a golden retriever hopped up next to me. I loved being that dog; the freedom, the belly rubs, there's nothing like it.

I looked across the theatre to my right and noticed the toddler sweetly playing with her doll. A pang of immense sadness grew in my heart. My poor mother. Watching her spirit slowly die along with my tiny, fragile body was the worst. Fuck cancer.

The room became dark as the screen in front of us flashed to white. Here we go. I watched my new self be born.

"Hey, our parents look wealthy, maybe I'll try out Harvard this round, get that master's degree in psychology we've always dreamed of." we all giggled at the thought.

I was going to be a boy this time, a *blond* boy. Interesting, I'm usually a brunette. Something was different, but I couldn't quite put my finger on it. Why were my eyes so dark? Are they always that dark after birth? A shiver ran down my spine.

We all sat in silence, patiently waiting to see who we would grow up to be. That's when I looked at me. I looked directly into the camera and gave the most sinister smile, almost as if, as if he, I, *knew*. How would that be possible though? We weren't allowed access to our old memories until we passed on.

The screen turned black and all at once the rest of my incarnations glanced in my direction. Eyes wide, mouth open, we were speechless. Normally we get to

PAST LIVES

see what our whole life entails, why was this different? I gave a small shrug and before I knew it, I was born.

Things are different this time, I remember everything, every life, every death, but it's almost as if I'm trapped inside my own mind. My thoughts have changed; I find myself fixating on details I never would have noticed in my past lives. Some days I have no feelings at all, while other days I feel everything at once, but on a heightened level. Like an itch I just can't seem to scratch.

I'm seventeen now and I have done things I wish I hadn't—horrible things. Poor Ducky, she was a good, loyal dog. I remember the soft kisses she gave me as I eagerly slit her throat. I remember the feeling it gave me to run my fingers through the warm blood. Why did she have to die?

To watch her bleed, the voice in my head taunts. Ah, that's right. I looked down in shame and understanding.

I'm at the park right now, watching, waiting. I watch as a child runs away from her mother, chasing after a butterfly. I used to enjoy life like that, back when I felt free, back when I was someone else. *Something* else. Back when I didn't fantasize about how much blood could pour out of a single vessel.

Now! Her! my inner demon hisses, interrupting my thoughts. I feel my body tense as a young woman passes by. My eyes instantly target in on her jugular, *I wonder if humans make the same gurgling sounds that animals do. I think I'll find out.*

Mr. Lakavote

$\mathcal{I}$'M NOT SURE IF THIS WILL HELP anyone, but if my story saves even one person from the nightmares I now endure, I will consider it a win. I have borrowed a phone that was smuggled in here, and the orderly that now monitors every move I make will be coming shortly, so I must be brief.

A few days ago, I was lying in bed scrolling through Reddit, like I always do to make myself sleepy, when I came across this story that sent shivers up my spine.

After I was done reading, I thought to myself, "wow, that was terrifying," and then scrolled to the next one. Big mistake.

Twenty minutes later I heard a scratching noise coming from my bedroom door and I froze. Confused as I live alone, I turned on the lamp next to me and looked towards my bedroom door.

Silence.

After a moment I decided it was my mind playing tricks on me. After all, I was reading scary stories in the dark. Probably not the best thing to do before bed, but hey, who doesn't love a good spine-chilling story before they close their eyes.

I went back to scrolling through the horror platform r/nosleep when again I heard a long scratch on the door. I slowly got out of bed and tip-toed over to the noise. Grabbing the door handle I gently opened it and peeked into my living room, only to find it vacant.

I quietly closed the door and turned to walk back towards my bed when my closet door flew open! Now, I don't know about you guys, but when it comes to fight or flight reaction, I seem to choose the option that leaves you frozen in place with your eyes closed. A defense mechanism instilled in me from childhood and stories of the boogeyman.

MR. LACKAVOTE

After a moment I decided to open my eyes and cautiously look towards my closet. I physically heard the clock that was placed on my nightstand stop ticking, and that's when I met him.

He was almost eight feet tall, standing on long spiny looking legs, with impossibly long arms that seemed to stretch on forever. What I could see of his body looked to be covered in deep dark cracks. He was wearing a long hooded cloak that touched the floor, as black as midnight on a moonless night, that slightly revealed his ruby red eyes.

"Wh—who are you?" I said with a shaky voice.

He never physically moved his mouth, but I heard him speak into my soul with the most sinister voice, "I am Mr. Lakavote and I am here to right your wrong."

Petrified and frozen in place, I tried to ask him what wrong I had done, but before I could finish, he was right in front of me. His breath smelled of rotting flesh and death itself as he breathed down my face.

He reached out and ran his long boney fingers across my cheek, and instantly I knew what he could do. I felt my eyes being ripped from my head and the burning sensation that followed. I began to scream, but no sound came out. I was stuck in my own personal hell as darkness surrounded me. Alone and afraid. I wanted to die. I wanted the agony to end.

Again, I heard his voice as if it were my own thoughts, "I am the keeper of votesss and you know what you did. You will right your wrong or I will take your eyesssss along with your eternal soul. You have twenty-four hoursss."

Just as fast as he had appeared, Mr. Lakavote had vanished.

I did not sleep the rest of the night. I had visions of the horror I had just endured that left me sweating and cold at the same time. Had I dreamt the whole thing? Could my mind even make up something so sinister and evil? And the pain, oh Lord the pain I felt, I have never experienced anything close to that kind of suffering in my entire life.

The next morning, pacing my apartment, I tried my hardest to think of what I had done wrong. Did I forget to vote in our recent election? Had I missed an employee poll at work? What the hell had I not voted on that was so important that my soul depended on it?

Trying to clear my head, I decided to open Reddit as it always seemed to make me feel better and relaxed. While I was scrolling, I passed the story I had read the night before. The one that had made the hair on the back of my neck stand.

That's when it clicked. I had scrolled to the next one before I gave that story the upvote it deserved. Instantaneously, I clicked on the up arrow and waited, hoping with every part of my being that, that was the answer. Was I playing a guessing game with my life?

I waited the whole day, I didn't eat, I didn't move, I barely even breathed. I thought about writing to my family and sorting my goodbyes out but, I felt too incredibly empty to conjure up the words. No one would believe me anyway.

As the sun slowly set, I decided I might as well wait in my room and hope that I had redeemed myself, or possibly chance losing my eyes and my soul. The thought of that alone made me vomit into the trash can next to my bed and tremble violently with deep, petrifying terror.

When my twenty-four-hour mark finally came, I closed my eyes, held my breath, and waited. Prayed. Begged to whoever was listening, that my soul would be saved, and all would be forgiven.

Silence.

Then, I heard the breathing, I smelled the rotting flesh, I felt all the hair on my body raise. When I finally opened my eyes, I felt a chill that froze me to the bone, as if I was sitting inside a freezer meant for the dead. There he was, right in front of me. His eyes had turned to sapphires as he stared into my soul.

"Don't let it happen again", he bellowed in a voice that to this day still haunts my dreams. Then he was gone.

I know some of you won't believe me. Hell, I'm not even sure if I believe myself. As the doctor here says, "it's all in my head". But, for the love of your eyeballs and your soul ... do *not* forget to vote while you are reading stories on Reddit, or you too will have the "pleasure" of meeting Mr. Lakavote for yourself.

The Tea Party

"Hurry up, Daddy! Natalie will be here any minute!"

I looked down to see my daughter, Bree, excitedly dancing in front of me. It was Sunday, which meant it was officially Tea Party day, and B was not about to let me forget it. I tried to tell her last week that she could invite any number of her friends over, but she only wanted Natalie. Her imaginary friend.

I watched as she bounded towards her room, pig tails flying behind her as the fake china clinked in her hands. I smiled as I closely followed with the teapot full of juice.

Once I reached her room, I noticed exactly three chairs set up; one for me, one for her, and one for

Natalie. I took my place in the largest chair while Bree very carefully began to pour the "tea" into our respective cups. Natalie's was purple of course, her favorite color.

"Dad, you should say hi to Natalie, it's rude to ignore her!" Bree retorted, as she poured my tea last.

"Oh, sorry honey. Uh, hi, Natalie, very happy to have you." I smiled at the empty chair. Bree giggled in return.

I'm sure most kids her age also have imaginary friends, but for some reason, Natalie concerned me. Bree had made up this very elaborate background story for her and, to put it lightly, it was disturbing.

Apparently, Natalie had grown up in a foster home her whole life, never having been able to stay longer than a few months at a time. "She has a lazy eye, and no one wants her because she's scary looking, but now she lives under our neighbor's basement," my little girl explained to me one night. It broke my heart to hear her makeup such a tale, maybe she wasn't taking this move as well as I had hoped.

I looked across the table at my sweet daughter talking enthusiastically to her special friend. I watched as she poured Natalie another glass of juice, mentally making a note that, that was in fact Bree's third glass and she would be needing to use the bathroom soon.

THE TEA PARTY

Moments later, upon Bree's request, I quietly excused myself to grab the crackers and cheese from the kitchen. I got about halfway down the hall when I heard her bathroom door shut.

Called it.

I returned shortly with a plate of crackers and cheese to find my daughter sitting sweetly in her chair. "Did you wash your hands sweetheart," I asked nonchalantly, trying not to embarrass her.

"Oh, I didn't use the bathroom daddy, Nat did, and yes, she washed her hands." Bree batted her big brown eyes at me.

I sighed. At least she washed her hands, I guess.

Once we were finished with our tea and crackers, Bree announced that Natalie had to go home now. I went through the whole charade of guessing where her coat was, while my little girl laughed at all my attempts before simply telling me where she had set it.

Holding the air in her hand, I watched her walk Natalie to our front door and hug her goodbye. Once she was satisfied that her friend had left, Bree turned onto her heels and ran towards the playroom, announcing she was going to color her a picture for next time.

I shook my head, oh to have that sort of imagination again. I turned to make my way to the kitchen, when I heard our doorbell ring. As I opened the door, I found my front porch empty. Just before I could close it again, I heard Bree yell at me from the other room.

"Natalie says she forgot her bracelet in my room. Can you grab it for her daddy?"

I looked at the empty space on my porch and decided to amuse my daughter. "

Uh, wait right here, Natalie," I yelled loud enough for Bree to hear. I walked back into her room and looked around the table, it was void of any bracelet. I chuckled to myself as I called out "ah, here it is."

Then, something caught my eye.

I glanced down at the purple teacup and noticed a shiny silver bracelet inside. My hands began to shake as I picked it up.

As I slowly turned it over, I saw the name "Natalie" delicately written on the inside.

You Don't Even Know

Yᴏᴜ ᴅᴏɴ'ᴛ ᴋɴᴏᴡ ᴡʜᴀᴛ's ɢᴏᴏᴅ ғᴏʀ you, do ya?

Just last week you were talking to that boring old lady across the street about the mundane happenings of life. How could you even relate to that peasant? I could tell by your body language you weren't enjoying the conversation; it was a pity talk. I put a stop to it right then and there.

The next time that old nobody even glances in your direction, she's going to get daggers from hell right into her clearance shelf soul. That will definitely teach her.

I frequently keep track of all of your friends, you never know who is real, and who just wants to climb that social latter. You would be surprised how many average joes try to hit on you, it's disgusting.

You see, I love you, I really do. You're the most beautiful person in the whole world and I feel sorry for everyone who has to exist around your radiance. People would kill to have half the sparkle you have; some have even tried I'm sure—I know I would.

That's why you keep me around, to help you know who is worthy and who isn't. I pick out her clothes, your food, even your schedule. You like to be your own boss, and with your talent, why shouldn't you? You're perfect.

Yesterday you had to deal with one of your friend's parents dying. I could see how that would be difficult, after all it was *your* birthday. How inconsiderate of your so-called pal to rain on your parade like that. So, I got rid of her.

I told her it would be great if we could go to lunch, *on your birthday, sorry about that*. She eagerly replied yes, like I knew she would.

There's an old warehouse about twenty miles out of town and no one heard her scream. I did of course. "Why are you doing this?" Was all she repeated over and over again. I did her a service really; she would get to see her dead father in no time. Like I said, she was so inconsiderate.

When I got home, I got the cake all ready and sat down to celebrate. You loved it. Of course, not too much, you need to really watch the figure. I tossed the rest in the garbage after you had small a slice, no need for temptation later on.

Next were the presents; a beautifully expensive gown you had your eye on for weeks, a Tiffany watch, and a new Coach purse. Only the best for the best; that's my motto. Also, couldn't have you prancing around with last year's designer bag though, #ew.

It was getting late and you needed your beauty sleep. After showering and exfoliating for exactly thirty minutes you hopped out and ran your hand across the foggy mirror. Now here you are in all your glory, just looking like a snack. I really do love our talks, you're the only one who will ever truly understand me.

Wouldn't it be so much easier if someone could just marry themselves? I know I'd definitely marry you. Like I said, you're perfect.

Nocturnal Nightmares

$\mathcal{I}$ HAD BEEN HAVING THE STRANGEST dreams lately that truly were starting to freak me out. Last month I woke up, sweat pouring down my face as I recalled the horrendous night terror.

A young woman was running for her life through a desolate wooded area. I could feel her fear deep in my bones as a set of hands wrapped around her neck, slowly causing her to fade into unconsciousness. When she awoke, she was strapped to a table as eager hands began to cut into her tender skin.

She tried to scream but no sound would come out. She tried to move but her body had been paralyzed from the neck down. She just watched as tears fell from her dirt stained cheeks, slowly gasping for air as life faded from her hazel eyes.

The next day I saw her picture on the news. Her lifeless body had been dumped on a frequently used jogging trail in the city. There were no leads in her murder, only the the star shaped mark etched into her skin by the killer.

It didn't stop there. Two weeks later I woke up screaming as I reached for my eyes.

Moments before, I had been in a dark room with the only light being casted from a swinging lamp above my head. Shadows danced along the walls like demons waiting for their master of death. In front of me was a young man, maybe in his early twenties. He was strapped to a chair with a dirty rag wrapped tightly around his mouth.

I heard the sound of a drill start causing my blood to run cold; I knew what was coming. I emerged from the shadows and swiftly moved to the man's side. Within seconds I watched a hand reach around his neck as the other one danced the drill above his eye. The rag muffled his cries of pain as the ever-twisting metal sunk into his socket, over and over; blood coated the demons, quenching their thirst for death.

Once again, I saw the familiar face on the new the following day. His body had been placed in the town fountain for all to see. A star had been scraped from the skin on his forehead.

Can you see my dilemma? Why do I have these terrible thoughts creep into my subconscious? Why do they keep coming true?

Last night was probably the worst of them all. My dream started out pleasant, I was walking along a trail when I ran into my old high school sweetheart. He hadn't aged a day from his prime. He grabbed me around the waist and dipped me down like you see in the movies. Leaning in for a long-lost kiss of destiny, when a hand reached up and slammed a needle into his neck.

Memories came flooding back to me as I recalled the horrible pain, he had put me through in our teen years. The bruises, the miscarriage, the lies. My heart ached as the stitches from my wounded pride began to rip open. I awoke with tears in my eyes. Not just for him, but for myself as well.

This morning I turned on the news expecting to see his face light up the screen. There were no alerts to be found. A sigh of relief escaped my lips as I turned off the TV. What a crazy thing to assume, I thought to myself. It's not like I can *actually* predict deaths.

Especially when the person was still in my basement, waiting to take his last breath.

Everyone Has Secrets, What's Yours?

$\mathcal{I}$ DON'T KNOW HOW LONG I HAVE BEEN here. Judging by the stomach pains and the stench of feces, my guess would be a day, maybe two.

The last thing I remember was being on the boardwalk with my girlfriends, having one too many drinks and spilling all the tea. I fell down a few times from the liquid courage; typical. "Breann you're so graceful," my friends mocked. I guess I get two left feet when inebriated, who doesn't?

I must have blacked out though because the next thing I remember is being in this box. When I woke up, I panicked. My breath turned into short spurts of anxiety as I screamed for help, no one heard. My throat felt like I had swallowed sand. Water. I needed water. It's so dark down here, so dark.

I felt around the limited space I was afforded when my hand hit a bottle. Praise be. I struggled to get it open as my hands trembled around the cap. I immediately poured the substance into my mouth, too thirsty to care if it was poison. It burned my esophagus as it went down. Vodka. *Why?*

I accepted the warm comfort of the spirit. My empty stomach however, heaved in response. Acid scorched my tongue like a yellow flame. I pounded on my wooden enclosure.

"Somebody *help* me," I cried. Tears fell down my cheeks like salty drops of betrayal.

I felt the floor vibrate as a dim light appeared near my feet. My phone! I scrambled my legs as adrenaline coursed through my veins. *Calm down Breann, you have to calm down,* I chanted in my head.

The air was thick and muggy. Sweat mixed with my tears as I tried to reach for the phone. Just a few more inches. After minutes of struggle I felt the cold metal on the tips of my fingers. Got it.

I pulled it to my face only to realize it wasn't mine. It appeared to be some sort of burner phone. I flipped it open and immediately tried to dial 911, it was no use, I couldn't make a call out. I clicked over to the message icon and my blood ran cold.

Hello, Breann. Do you want to play a game?

What. The. Fuck.

My fingers grasped onto the device until I thought they might bleed. Cursing under my breath, I punched in my reply.

Who the fuck is this? I shook with anger. My phone lit up almost immediately.

Wrong answer.

I held my breath, as I felt my encloser begin to shake. Before I had the chance to comprehend what was happening, I was weightless. The box began to drop quickly along with my stomach. I heard a sharp snap like a whip and then it was over. My heart was racing in my chest. I wasn't below ground; I was above it; *way* above it.

I gasped for air and begged my body to settle while I brought the phone back up to my face.

Now that I have your attention … Let's play, shall we? Do you know why you are here?

My heart sank into my chest. I had no fucking idea why someone would want to do this to me. I began to sob at the thought of falling again. My fingers traced the letters I would reply. I closed my eyes and hit send.

No. Please. I'm so scared. I begged. My phone shook in my hand.

Wrong answer.

I closed my eyes and inhaled sharply waiting for the drop. The box remained still. I screamed into the darkness as my phone lit up again.

I'm sure Bella was just as scared as you are right now. The words cut into me like I dull knife.

Bella. More tears began to fall. Bella was a little girl that I used to babysit. She passed away two years ago, but it wasn't my fault, there was nothing I could have done.

"God, it wasn't my fault," I yelled as I pounded my fist into the wood above my head.

Wrong answer.

The box dropped again, further this time; I pissed myself on the descent. My whole body began to tremble in shock.

"What do you want from me?" I yelled.

Confess.

I cried out into the void. Begged for someone to hear, for someone to save me from this hell. I took a deep breath when I was answered with silence. I brought the phone back up to my face and exhaled.

I had been drinking. I'm so sorry. I lost control of the vehicle and we went into the river. I tried ... I tried to save her. I promise. I swear I tried. I gripped the phone in my sweaty palm and waited.

Wrong. Answer.

A timer started flashing on the phone when I started typing this, and I don't know what it means. The box is swaying back and forth, and I have drunk the rest of the vodka. It wasn't much, but enough to calm the nerves.

The timer is at five minutes now and if this is the end, I need to confess. I didn't try to save Bella. I could have, but I was too scared and decided to save myself instead. I don't know if anyone will read this, but I needed to get it out. I needed to confess.

I have one-minute left. I'm so sorry. I'm just so sorrrrrrrrrrrrrrr—

✳✳✳

My name is Grace and I am a detective for the beautiful city of Seattle. Yesterday, I received an anonymous phone call giving me the directions to a murder scene, but my nine years on the job did not prepare me for what I would find.

Shards of broken pieces of wood were sprawled across the pavement, along with bits of flesh and viscera. Given the appearance and stench of the melted goo, the heat had not been kind the last few days.

My hand flew up to my mouth as I made my way over to the pancake before me. A reflection from a piece of metal caught the sun just right, catching my attention. I looked down and noticed a hand tightly wrapped around a phone. I put on some gloves and pried the bloated appendages from the device before opening it up.

The first thing I read is what I have typed above. For any of this to make sense, you needed to know. The next thing I read caused goosebumps to spread over my entire body.

Hello, Detective Grace. On this device you will find the full confession of Breann Marie for the murder of Bella Mitchell.

Breann is the first of many. Everyone has secrets detective … and they need to confess.

The Hangman is coming, and he tends to collect.

The Shadows of Sunny Hollow

$\mathcal{I}$ AM A CAREGIVER WORKING IN AN assisted living home for seniors. I absolutely love my job and the clients I care for, but I fear I may not return after what happened tonight.

It was bedtime at Sunny Hollows Senior Home and all of my clients were going about their routines as per usual. A warm cup of tea for Sandra, a melatonin for Peter, and a five-minute meditation for Jil; the schedule was going perfectly.

Around eight o'clock all of them had retired to their bedrooms, where they would stay until early dawn. Doors were shut, blinds were drawn, the house was ready for rest. I was making my way to the kitchen to clean up the dinner mess when I heard footsteps slowly creep down the hall toward the client's rooms.

"Jil darling, did you need something?" I called out, expecting to see her waddling back to her room from one last restroom visit.

Silence.

I curiously walked towards the hall and stopped dead in my tracks. Standing in her doorway was a dark shadow. I couldn't see its eyes, but as it rocked back and forth, I felt as if it was staring at me, taunting me. Goosebumps rose up my arms like tiny ghostly pimples feasting on my fears.

The sound of drums beat heavily in my ears. I pulled my hands up to my temples and watched as the shadow mimicked my movement.

I tried to find my voice when a lamp turned on from inside the room. The shadow vanished.

"Harmony, can you please shut my door?" Jil called out in a groggy voice.

I instantly snapped back into reality, "Of course Jil, on my way."

I tiptoed down the hall and peeked inside of her room; she was still snuggled in bed and giving me quite the annoyed look. I smiled meekly and slowly closed her door. My breath quickened as I made my way back to the kitchen, butterflies twisting throughout my stomach the whole way.

The rest of the shift was uneventful. I finished the evening chores then sat down to debrief the night with a book. Around ten o'clock, the graveyard crew walked through the door which meant I could go home; I was relieved.

I walked out into the brisk night, the smell of spring heavy in the air as the cherry blossoms danced in the wind. I fumbled with my car keys, not able to shake the feeling of being watched. I quickly climbed into the cab of my Suburban and started her up.

As the engine warmed, I glanced just behind Sunny Hollow. There was a native burial ground a block away, could that explain the experience I had? I shook my head and sighed. Why do I let these thoughts encompass my mind?

I put my car into gear and drifted forward. I got maybe two feet when everything shut off: the engine, the lights. I was encased by darkness. I reached for the door handle, but it wouldn't budge; I was trapped from the inside.

My heart began to pound rapidly in my chest. I hate closed spaces. I reached for my phone to call for help when something caught my eye. There was a shadow staring at me from Jil's bedroom window.

Tingles crept up my spine as I sat in my trance. The shadow leaned closer to the glass, the moon proudly shining on its smile with a sinister glow. Inhaling sharply through my teeth, I pushed myself into the passenger seat. Sitting with my back against the door I fumbled for my phone, eyes locked on the shadow.

I felt the rubber case tickle my fingertips and quickly glanced down to retrieve it from my purse. When I looked back towards the window, the shadow was gone. I exhaled slowly, trembling as I brought my phone up to my face.

Click.

The locks beckoned me to exit the vehicle, causing me to jump at the sound. I reached over and turned the key; the engine roared back to life. Scooting back into the driver's seat I got the hell out of there.

On the ride home I began to feel heavy. A dark cloud of anxiety had taken over, causing my head to spin. I pulled into my driveway and stumbled out onto the grass; sleep was beginning to cloud my eyes.

Opening my door, I was greeted by my enthusiastic shepherd, Friedan. She was bouncing up and down, happy I was home, until she looked behind me. My normally peaceful friend immediately froze, hair on end as she let out a deep growl.

I took a step back, confused at her random outburst. She pushed past my legs, hackles still up as she stared hard at the wall.

"What are you barking at, crazy? It's just my shadow." I patted her on the head.

Then something moved from behind me. I turned around just in time to watch my shadow move up the wall until it was right above my head. Peering down at me with outstretched arms, it danced to a nonexistent flame.

Terror washed over me. The shadow had followed me home, and I think it intends to stay.

Women Must Serve Men

Growing up in a very religious home, I was taught that women must always serve men. Given the fact we were created from a man's rib, it only made sense that we were put on this earth to be companions for them.

I often used to dream about the day I would find my partner. *Would he be handsome? Would he be strong but gentle? Would he be my provider and protector?* My young mind had no idea what the years would bring.

When I turned eighteen, I met John. He was everything I could have imagined and more. Sweet, gentle, kindhearted; he was perfect. We had an advantageous marriage per the request of my parents, and it was magical. Winter had come and encased the grounds with a vast blanket of divine white powder, causing us to light several fires in its midst. The warm glow beckoned our guests with a dance of ice and fire.

The ceremony was beautiful. Our family dog, Kenai even brought our rings down the aisle, gliding swiftly between the stones. John expressed his ever-dying love for me in front of all our family and friends, and just like that, we were husband and wife.

We set off for our honeymoon hours after and quickly boarded the plane to Bora Bora; a beautiful gift from his parents. The first day was perfect. We spent all of our time wrapped in each other's arm, filled with all the love our bodies could muster. I remember gazing into his dark brown eyes of heaven, asking myself how I got so lucky. Then his whole demeanor changed.

I watched as his mood slowly shifted, the moment I mentioned our future children.

"Let's just hope our first is a boy," he remarked. I stared back at him confused, why would the sex of our baby matter? I chalked it up to the fact that all men must dream of having a boy first, to carry on their legacy and last name.

WOMEN MUST SERVE MEN

The next day however, his true feelings began to show. While at breakfast I watched as he ordered *for* me, mortified not only at his selection, but also at the authority that dripped heavily on his tongue. The rest of the day stayed true to the morning; no choices made that day were my own.

When our honeymoon was over, things progressed immensely. I found that he thought my friends were childish and that I should make new ones. He also forcibly mentioned that I should quit my job and remain home, a request that when refused, resulted in pain and dark sunglasses.

I begged my parents for help, pleaded with them to talk with John, but I always received the same reply.

"You must serve your husband, Danielle." I would cry for many sleepless nights when I found out I was pregnant with our daughter.

John was furious.

"How could you give me such a weak child?" he would yell at me with such a darkness in his eyes, I feared for my life. I had to find a way to protect my baby from his wrath.

My parents had given us Kenai as a wedding present, my one true companion in this dark world shaped by men. He collected most of my fear born tears with his obsidian fur; always there, always comforting.

Last night John came home in one of his moods, destined to set my world aflame with his hands. I took blow after blow before something changed in Kenai's eyes; he had, had enough.

With the strength of a dragon he rose from his bed, eyes locked onto John's throat. One moment, he had his hand clasped tightly around my throat, the next he was reaching for his own as Kenai tore into the chauvinistic flesh.

I fell to the floor, hands covering my eyes as I heard my husband scream out in pain. The sound of blood gurgling in his throat serenaded the night; I was free. When Kenai had finished with his prey, he pranced over to me with a warmth I had almost forgotten.

With shaking legs, I crawled to John, a part of me hoping he was alive, while the other rejoiced in his departure. When no pulse was to be found, I leaned heavily against the couch and sighed. *How was I supposed to get rid of the body?*

Today I woke up to a text from my mother asking John and I to attend my younger brother's graduation BBQ. A brief moment of panic coursed through my veins, before the solution hit me in the gut like the betrayal of a knife.

WOMEN MUST SERVE MEN

I spent a few hours preparing a dish for the celebration, while Kenai danced at my feet. I made sure to throw him a few pieces as a reward for his bravery. Once everything was ready, we departed to my parent's house.

I informed my family that John was ill and wanted me to send them all of his love. They bought it. When dinner was placed on the table below the cherry blossoms, I glanced around at my family with joy in my heart.

"Wow Danielle, this meat is so tender and delicious. You must tell me your recipe," my aunt smiled at me with a mouthful of food. I beamed up at her and nodded as I patted Kenai from under my chair.

I looked down at my plate with pride. I had done my duty as a wife despite all of my tribulations.

After all, women must *serve* men.

Acknowledgments

I would like to thank everyone who helped me on this project.

✶**Nick Botic** for his editing, guidance, and teaching me how to publish on my own!

✶**Edyth Pax-Boyr** for typesetting and making this book look as good as it possibly could. Seriously, wow!

✶**Aina and Christian Tolero** for their gorgeous illustrations!

✶**Victoria Davies** for a cover straight out of my dreams!

Thank you so, so much. Without any one of you this collection would not be half as amazing as it is, and I am so eternally grateful.

About the Author

Melody Grace is a writer of all things terrifying and unsettling. She began her journey to the dark side at a very young age as a way to bring her fears to life. Now, being a mother herself, she found out that there is actually nothing scarier than crotch goblins; little creatures that you willingly give your heart and soul to … forever.

Terrifying, isn't it?

While the handsome little goblin is asleep, she often finds solitude in writing while sipping some red wine and enjoying the beautiful weather in the Pacific Northwest.

As you read her stories, you will find that her dreams are now your nightmares as she sweeps you into her dark realm.

Manufactured by Amazon.ca
Acheson, AB